The Billionaire's Terms

Elizabeth Lennox

Table of Contents

Chapter 1

Alicia stared at her reflection in her bedroom mirror, her eyes widening in shock. "No way, Maggie. I can't wear this," she said to her younger sister, starting to pull the beautiful, but sexy red, slip dress off her slim shoulders. She had an odd feeling something momentous was going to happen tonight and she was wondering if she wanted that to happen in such a daring dress.

Maggie put her hands on her older sister's shoulders, laughing at the horrified expression. "Yes you can. You look fabulous and I can guarantee that other people will be wearing much more revealing dresses than this. You'll stand out if you wear something as conservative that," she explained, her hand waving to the boring, black crepe dress Alicia had originally been planning to wear. "Besides, you don't have an alternative. It is the only fancy dress I have and you don't have any. Your black dress isn't appropriate for this kind of a function. Trust me."

Alicia sighed. Her sister was right. She didn't have any other option but that didn't stop her hands from moving to the spaghetti straps to pull the bodice slightly higher. She was biting her lower lip in indecision, worrying about so many things that might or might not happen. The possibilities were daunting and terrifying.

Sighing heavily, Alicia shook her head. "I think I'll just skip the event," she started to say, turning away from the mirror.

"Absolutely not!" Maggie replied emphatically and moved around to face her sister, blocking her view of the dress in the mirror. Looking right into Alicia's dark blue eyes, she smiled. "Alicia, this is your big

1

night. You are always so focused on working and rarely get out for just a fun night. Go out, have a good time and just relax with your friends. It is a company party, not a death sentence, so all of your co-workers will be there. It will be seen as a slight by your peers if you don't attend."

Alicia's shoulders drooped, knowing her sister was right. Her coworkers were looking forward to tonight and had been talking about it for weeks.

She wished she had some sort of emergency that would suddenly pop up and get her out of tonight. She hated going to these kinds of functions on her own. "Yes, but they all have husbands or significant others. I'll be all alone," she said, worried about going, as well as the consequences of not going.

Maggie smiled encouragingly. "You'll be fine. Just pretend you're royalty and they'll all assume you know something they don't. You'll fascinate them." Maggie chuckled at her sister's curious expression and continued. "Just consider this the beginning of your freedom from the past ten years. Good grief, you've been working at least three jobs for so long to help mom and me, no wonder you're nervous about going out and just relaxing."

Alicia considered her sister's comments and peered around to inspect her image again. Maggie was right. Where was the old Alicia? The one that had hung out with friends and laughed and relaxed? She'd been smothered by responsibility and...and exhaustion.

Tonight...it might be fun to just get out and laugh. To talk with her coworkers without thinking about the next assignment or problem.

Still, she bit her lower lip as she surveyed her appearance in the mirror. "Are you sure this dress isn't too risqué?" she asked nervously even as her heart fluttered with an old sensation. Excitement? Yes, that was it. She used to be so carefree and...and hopeful!

Maggie shook her head firmly. "You know it isn't. I wore it to that dinner two weeks ago and no one even blinked. So stop worrying about it and just go out to enjoy yourself. You definitely deserve it," she urged.

Accepting that Maggie wasn't going to take no for an answer

and her younger sister really did have a knack for dressing with style, Alicia laughed and hugged her sister. "Okay, you've taken away every one of my arguments. So I'll go but I'm only going to make an appearance, then get right back out of there. I'm not the social butterfly like you are. Not anymore, at least." She groaned. "You can talk to just about anyone and get their life history out of them. It's why you're so good at your job," she said, referring to Maggie's month-old job as an aide to a senator down in Washington, D.C.

Maggie shook her head, denying her sister's assertion that the social aspect of work life was too hard. "You'll be fine. Just smile occasionally and I guarantee that the men will do the rest," she assured her, eyeing her sister's beautiful, delicate features dominated by her blue, almond shaped eyes that shone like cat eyes out of a creamy complexion that a model would die for. Throw in her lustrous brown locks that hung down over her shoulders, and Alicia was a stunning woman. And what's more, she didn't know it, nor did she care. A more selfless woman, Maggie had never known.

Snapping out of her inspection, she picked up a brush. "Let's do something with that hair, shall we?" she said and pushed Alicia into a chair so she could tackle her thick, long, brown hair that curled just slightly at the ends.

"Good luck," Alicia grumbled, but gave in to the tender ministrations of Maggie.

After a half hour, Maggie had achieved a miracle. "How's that?" she asked, stepping out of the way so Alicia could see her hair in the mirror.

Instead of the thick hair that just fell in waves down her back, Maggie had pulled it all into a pony tail then curled the ends so they twirled in corkscrews down her back leaving small tendrils floating around her face.

Alicia's mouth almost fell open at the image staring back at her from the mirror. "Maggie, I can't believe you! This is amazing," she whispered, turning her face to the right and left to see the effect. "I feel like a supermodel," she laughed. "Where did you learn to do this?"

Maggie smiled and tossed the brush down onto the beaten dressing table. "In college, our study group would do each other's hair while quizzing each other. We got into some serious competitions on both hair and grades."

Maggie was being humble. She'd received straight A's through-out college in every single class. "Well, it worked. You're brilliance is evident with your skills at hair styling as well as academically."

"And to top it off, here's cab fare," Maggie said.

Alicia stared at the cash, instantly uncomfortable. "Maggie...."

Her younger sister took Alicia's hand and stuffed the bills into it, closing her fingers over the cash immediately. "Don't even try it," she admonished. "You're not going to mess up this hairstyle by walking and I'm not letting you take the New York City subway at night, not dressed like that," she admonished. "Besides, you put me through college and now I have a great job. Allow me to pay back some of what you sacrificed all those years for me."

Alicia opened her fingers and stared at the money, swallowing the lump in her throat as her emotions threatened to overwhelm her. "You don't have to do this," she told her sister.

Maggie smiled gently. "Neither did you, but you did it anyway. For ten years you supported me and mom after dad's...." she stopped, leaving an uncomfortable pause as the two sisters pushed painful memories aside. "Well, you know," she finished weakly. "Please, let me do this small thing for you. Take the money and have a great time tonight."

Alicia relented, grateful to her sister, hugging Maggie to show her how much she loved her. "I'll be back early," she said. "We'll go out for breakfast tomorrow morning to splurge before you have to head back to Washington, D.C."

"Deal," Maggie said, smiling broadly.

Chapter 2

Adam Meyers laughed at the odd joke his vice president had just told while at the same time surveying the crowd, assessing the party-goers with a critical eye. The party was apparently a huge success and he should congratulate the coordinators. This year's company spring ball had turned out nicely.

Excusing himself, he shifted away from the group he'd been in to circulate further, he was scanning the crowd in search of Nancy Yost, head of Human Relations and this year's coordinator when his eyes and senses were captured by a knockout figure encased in a stunning red dress. For a long time, Adam's eyes just took in the luscious figure, amazed that he hadn't seen her before now. She was surrounded by several other men so perhaps that's the reason. He wondered which one was her date for the night. Whoever it was, the man was certainly lucky, he thought to himself. Was it the guy now leading her onto the dance floor?

"What's the news on the latest proposal, Adam?" Jim Lewis asked, Vice President of Business Development.

Adam ignored the man talking to him, knowing that the other man was just schmoozing. Having built up his company from nothing into a multi-billion dollar conglomerate, he had no patience for people trying to flatter their way into his good graces.

Actions and accomplishments were what he recognized in people. A few moments ago, Adam had been only mildly amused at the man's ambitions but he had no problem cutting him off by turning his back on the man without any further pleasantries when the man started

5

schmoozing. Adam rarely had time for petty chit chat. There was always something more important to discuss. He had no remorse for the man or his fawning. The woman in the red dress was all that held his interest now.

Adam watched as the woman thanked her latest partner and walked off the dance floor. He was so transfixed by the woman's movements, it took him a long time to realize that she was actually trying to leave.

"Oh, no," Adam muttered under his breath. "You put yourself out there, looking incredibly lovely and way too tempting. There's no way you're going to leave now."

Adam quickly picked up two glasses of champagne from a passing waiter and moved toward the woman with single minded purpose. His employees knew better than to stop him in this mode so he was able to move towards the door unencumbered.

Alicia glanced around, feeling less awkward than she had anticipated, but still ready to call it a night. She'd arrived two hours ago and found her co-workers. They were a fun group, constantly pushing a glass of wine or champagne into her hands and filling up her plate. Unfortunately, Alicia was too nervous to eat but the wine was wonderful and she sipped it just to have something to do with her hands. Now, her head was feeling a little fuzzy and she knew it was time to leave.

"Leaving so soon?" a deep voice called out from behind her.

Alicia turned around, her lips curling into a polite smile, but ready to excuse herself. She was tired and had accomplished her mission for the evening.

However, her mind stopped functioning when she looked up into the stranger's face. He was, without doubt, the most gorgeous man she'd ever met in her life. He smiled down at her with dark, almost black eyes from a height of well over six feet. His shoulders were so broad, he blocked out her view of the rest of the ballroom but his smile was what caught her attention the most. It was devastating.

He placed one hand under her elbow, maneuvering her so they were blocked by the wall on one side and his broad shoulders on the other. "Please say you're not leaving. It isn't yet midnight," he teased. "Even Cinderella stayed until then."

Alicia flushed, wishing she could come up with a witty reply. But all she could manage was a breathless, "Cinderella wasn't up at five-thirty this morning."

He raised one eyebrow in question at her response. "What on earth were you doing up that early in the morning?" he asked, putting a hand on her arm as a couple moved by them.

Each time he touched her, an electric jolt shot right through her, straight to her stomach. Alicia's arm was on fire with his simple touch. Her skin tingled and she could only stare at his hands, wondering how she could feel so much from just a gentle, protective gesture.

She looked up into his face and noticed that his eyes were waiting on a response. "Oh, just cleaning my apartment," she said quickly, filling in the silence.

One dark eyebrow went up at her reply in astonishment. "At five-thirty in the morning?" he asked. "Surely someone as beautiful as you had something much better to do that early in the morning," he said, flashing another charming, sexy smile that instantly increased Alicia's heart rate tenfold.

Alicia told herself to snap out of her trance. She flushed, wondering what he was thinking she should be doing so early in the morning. "Well, um....not really," she said awkwardly and took a long swallow of the ice cold champagne he'd handed her a moment ago, hoping the cold liquid would quench her suddenly dry throat.

"Come dance with me," he said, and put their glasses on a passing waiter's tray He didn't wait for a response, but simply put his hand to the small of her back and guided her onto the dance floor.

Alicia didn't have the will to say no. Nor did she want to, she realized when he enfolded her gently in his strong, muscular arms. He danced wonderfully, she thought as he guided her to the music, the wine she'd drunk over the past couple of hours was relaxing her enough so she wasn't making a complete cake of herself as this overwhelmingly gorgeous man smiled down at her.

"You're a good dancer," she said, trying to come up with something to say.

His dark eyes watched her features, his chuckle indicating his surprise at her tone. "Why do you sound surprised?"

She laughed softly. "You wouldn't ask me that if you were my feet." Leaning forward conspiratorially, she whispered. "The other men here tonight aren't as talented," she explained.

"I noticed you enjoyed a large group of men's attentions tonight," he replied.

Alicia was surprised that he'd noticed her dancing with the other men.

"Yes, well, everyone has been very nice," she said, looking over his shoulder awkwardly.

Adam chuckled. "I don't think any man holding you in his arms would like to be considered 'nice'," he argued, his dark eyes looking into her blue ones, seeming to be able to see into her soul and know how he was affecting her blood pressure and her racing heart.

Alicia blushed. "Well, you know what I mean," she said, almost stuttering now that he was looking at her so intensely. She started to pull out of his arms. But his arms stopped her. "I'd better head out."

"Oh, no, lovely one. I finally have you in my arms, I'm going to keep you here for at least one song."

Alicia smiled shyly and stopped trying to pull away. What harm could one dance have? And it was so nice to be held in his strong arms. Her fingers were lightly touching the soft material of his tuxedo but she could feel the muscles regardless. Not only was he tall and handsome, but he was built too!

The song finally ended and Alicia was about to thank him for the dance and walk away, not wanting to be one of those mooning females that didn't get the hint. But he stopped her yet again. "Come have some champagne with me," he urged, taking her hand and guiding her outside onto the deserted balcony.

Alicia knew she shouldn't be out here alone with this man. He made her think thoughts that were better left un-thought. His chiseled face and charming smile told her that he was definitely out of her league.

But he wouldn't let her go and, to be honest with herself, she didn't want to go. She took the glass of champagne he handed her, taking a long sip.

"Thank you," she said and walked to the edge of the balcony with him, looking out into the inky black sky.

"What are you doing here alone?"

The darkness and the champagne were making her brave. "Who says I'm alone?" she asked, looking up at him from beneath her lashes.

The amusement was there in his dark, mysterious eyes. "Because if you were here with another man, then he's a fool and I'd be asking you why you were with him. But since you're not with someone else, answer my original question."

She disagreed, but was flattered that he thought a man would be silly to leave her alone. "Perhaps I enjoy being alone."

A dark eyebrow lifted at that comment, then he shook his head. "Nonsense. Why would you be trying to flee the party so early?"

"Because I'm tired?" she asked, hoping he would just leave it at that and move on.

"You're wide awake now," he pointed out.

Alicia took another long swallow of her drink and looked up at him. He really was incredibly handsome and made her stomach flutter with his dark look that promised secrets that only he could give her. "I think that has more to do with the company than with my physical state."

"I'm flattered," he said and clinked her glass. "The next question is, why don't you have a boyfriend?"

9

Alicia drank the rest of her glass nervously. How could she admit to this handsome and incredibly sophisticated man that she had been too busy waitressing and working retail jobs to pay for her sister's college and her mother's mortgage? She hadn't had the time or energy to have any life up until a few weeks ago.

And then something amazing occurred to her. Something Maggie had been trying to tell her earlier tonight. She was twenty-six years old and was now free of some overwhelming burdens. Why couldn't she just relax and have a little fun? Especially with this man? What harm could a little flirtation have? She knew it was the alcohol talking but she didn't care.

Her eyes suddenly sparkled with mischief and she faced him fully, not wanting to appear skittish anymore.

"Why don't you have a girlfriend?" she countered, coming out of her normally shy state to challenge the man. "You're handsome and probably smart, although I don't have any evidence of that at this point. Surely you could charm some lady to keep you company."

His eyebrows went up at her change in demeanor but he obviously liked the change. "Who says I'm here alone?"

Alicia smiled and threw his answer right back at him. "Because if you were here with another woman, then she's a fool and I'd be asking you why you were with her."

Adam threw back his head and laughed. "Touché," he replied. "But men don't want clingy women."

"And women like clingy men? That's very sexist of you, sir." A sudden thought startled her and she straightened abruptly. "I'm sorry, I've been standing here talking to you and dancing with you but I have no idea what your name is. I'm Alicia," she said, her smile widening at the realization that she'd been with this man for almost forty-five minutes and didn't even know his name.

"The name's Adam, and in men, it is called being protective, not clingy. Besides, I never denied being a sexist," he replied with an unrepentant grin.

She smothered a laugh. "Well, Adam, that's very disappointing. I would have thought you were a modern man with more enlightened views."

"Sorry to disappoint you," he said and took another glass of champagne from a passing waiter, handing it to her.

Alicia smiled her thanks and looked up at him, definitely relaxed now. In fact, she felt almost as if she were floating on a cloud. She wasn't sure if it was the champagne or the gorgeous man in front of her, blatantly flirting with her but she didn't really care. She felt better than she had in a long time and she didn't want that feeling to end.

"I doubt you'd ever be able to disappoint a woman," she said, then realized what she'd said. Straightening awkwardly, she was grateful that the darkness hid the fierce blush staining her cheeks. "I mean.... um...well," she stuttered, completely flustered.

Adam just smiled wickedly and leaned forward so he was whispering in her ear. "I've had no complaints so far," he said quietly, his lips brushing her earlobe, causing a shiver to race down her body and her breath to stop in her throat.

"Yes, well," she said breathily, all thoughts leaving her head completely at his touch. She cleared her throat and took another long sip of the bubbly liquid, staring at the button in the middle of his shirt front, hoping he didn't feel the tremor that shook her whole body. "I'll take your word for it," she whispered and took another long swallow of the sparkling wine.

"What? No challenge back?" Adam challenged, moving closer, so close she had to move her glass to her side or her hand would be touching his shirt.

He took her glass and put it behind her on the cement banister.

"Adam," she whispered, "this probably isn't the best place to do this," she said, but her eyes looked up to his, hoping he would kiss her so she would know what it felt like. His lips seemed firm and commanding, as if he could will her to kiss him back.

"Adam!" a shrill voice said from the balcony doorway interrupting whatever was about to happen. Alicia jumped back, uncomprehending of what sort of freakish animal had interrupted their darkness and aborted their kiss with such a jarring voice.

Adam's mouth twisted into a grim smile and she felt his hands tighten slightly on her waist. "Caught," he whispered before he released her and turned to greet whoever had found their private spot. "Good evening, Martha. How are you tonight?" he asked, putting an arm around Alicia and greeting the woman with a polite smile.

They chatted with the woman and a few others who wandered out to the balcony for several minutes. Finally, Adam excused them and pulled Alicia back into the ballroom, bringing her closer into his arms and looking down at her as he started dancing again.

"I'm guessing you didn't want to talk to them?" Alicia said, her body melting into his strong, powerful one.

"No," Adam replied, his eyes heavy lidded as he took in her features one by one. "I don't want to talk." His voice was deep and husky, leaving no miscommunication as to what he wanted.

"Ah," was all she could say, licking her lips as a dangerous thrill shot through her with his look. She simply smiled up into his sexy eyes, elated that he wanted to be with her instead of some other more glamorous or sophisticated woman. The look he gave her made her feel powerful and sexy, but very feminine, and his hand moving along her spine sent shivers throughout her body she couldn't hide from his knowing touch.

"Come with me tonight," he said.

Alicia's smile widened, feeling very feminine with the knowledge that he wanted her. It was such a novel experience, she wanted to savor it. She also knew she couldn't do anything about it. "No, I don't believe I'm the one-night-stand kind of woman," she said, but again, she was overjoyed that he would offer.

"Who says it has to be a one night stand?" he asked, twirling her and keeping her slightly off balance so she had to lean into him to stay on her feet.

Alicia laughed throatily, wondering how she could feel so secure in his arms while at the same time feel so nervous about what he was proposing. "Adam, don't kid yourself. Although I'm flattered, I'm definitely not your type."

He smiled charmingly as he pulled her closer into a spin on the dance floor. "What's my type?"

"Hmmm....models, actresses, social women who know how to play the game. I don't fit into any of those categories, unfortunately."

"Why unfortunately?"

"Because I'm thinking you would be a wonderful lover," she sighed, smiling up at him, unsure where she gathered the courage to flirt like this. She'd always been incredibly reserved around men. Tonight was different, her mind accepting the crazy feelings racing through her. Whatever the reason, she shook her head when he smiled.

"But you're determined to not find out, aren't you?" he said.

"That's correct," she said and slid her hand up around his shoulders, her fingers delicately touching his soft, black hair. "But I thank you for making me feel beautiful tonight. You definitely are just the boost my confidence needed."

Alicia didn't realize it, but he had casually danced them over to another balcony, this one on the side that was shrouded in darkness. As soon as they were close, Adam took her gently by the hand and led her out into the cool night.

By the time they had reached the doors, Alicia found herself wrapped in an embrace that might have been of her own doing. But Wow! His lips were firm and definitely commanded all of her attention. She felt the cement of the building against her back as he leaned her against the wall, his hands exploring her waist, moving upwards to rest just under her breast. The night air, the noise from the people inside and the music were all gone. Only this man, his hands and his mouth, were present in her mind along with intense, terrifyingly passionate feelings this man evoked within her. Nothing else.

Within moments, Alicia's shock wore off and she was kissing

him back with just as much fervor. Her hands moved from his shoulders to his chest, slipping underneath the fine wool of his tuxedo to touch the muscles just underneath the silk shirt.

He pulled her away from the building and held her in his arms, one hand coming up to hold her head while the other pulled her body closer to his. Alicia could no longer think as her body's feelings took over. Each touch of his mouth as it slanted over hers was like instant heat shooting right to her core, building up and then shooting back to her mouth to take as much as she was giving.

The heat inside her was becoming painful and she wanted more. The dizzy feeling she had was no longer because of the champagne but only because of his hands and his mouth which left hers to travel along her jaw and move slowly to her ear. His tongue and teeth teased the lobe, touching and nibbling along the shell of her ear, then traveling down to find the sensitive place on her neck she never knew existed.

It was a slow, sultry kiss that never seemed to end. He heard the voices close by and pulled away, taking a large step back just as another couple strolled out into their private area. This time, the other couple didn't speak to them, barely noticed them as they moved slowly to the opposite end of the balcony, lost in a private joke between the two of them. Neither of them noticed Alicia breathing heavily, desperately trying to get hold of her emotions and her body as Adam stared at her, one hand sliding into his pocket which only made him look like some sort of movie star.

But there was no one in the background to shout "Cut" or to ease the burning inside her that only intensified as Adam pulled her hand into his and guided her out of their hiding place and back into the noisy ballroom. He didn't stop, but he simply waved his hand cordially as they passed several people obviously determined to speak with him.

Adam pulled her along, not roughly but with determination, straight into a waiting limousine. As soon as they were settled inside and he barked the command, "Home," to the driver, he shut the glass partition and took her back into his arms.

Alicia only shivered in fear for a moment before giving in to the sinful pleasure that his hands and his mouth could give her. And she felt more free to explore him as well now that they weren't about to be discovered by so many other people.

After only a short drive, the driver stopped in an underground parking lot and Adam opened the door, solicitously helped her out of the car and quickly guided her into the waiting elevator. He punched a code and the elevator smoothly started moving.

He turned back to face her, his dark eyes searching her blue ones intently. "Are you sure you want this?" he asked, his hands loosely holding her waist as he watched the expressions on her face, making her understand exactly what was going to happen.

Alicia smiled gently, her hand reaching up to touch his handsome face, letting her fingers feel the power in his jaw and the softness in his determined mouth. A half hour ago, she would have said absolutely not and run from the building. But after being in his arms and experiencing the magic of his burning, heated kiss, she knew that this was the only place she wanted to be, the only place that was necessary at this point in time. Her mind wasn't sure if it was the smartest place to be but her body didn't care.

"Yes," Alicia said, her hands sliding up the black wool again, her fingers diving into his hair to pull his head back down to hers. As long as he was kissing her, her misgivings about what was going to happen evaporated. She wanted this like nothing else she'd ever wanted in her life. She briefly thought of the past ten years, of doing everything that was good and right and expected of her. And then Adam's hand slid higher along her waist, his hand touching her breast through the thin material of her dress and her whole body arched, her head thrown back and her breath catching in her throat.

"You're so beautiful," Adam said, his voice husky as he watched the emotions fly across her face, his hand briefly touching her pebbled nipple, then moving quickly away as if taunting the sensitive peaks. His body was already rock hard, had been since he'd taken her into his arms several hours ago but now there was an urgency about his need. Her mouth was open and her breathing rapid and as his hand explored. Small, sexy little moans escaped from her, turning him on even more.

Adam had been with women in the past but never had he picked up a woman from a party and left with her. His moral code demanded that he know a woman before he slept with her. He was no wallflower and had been with women in the past. Many women in fact. And he tried to put this one, tiny woman with her sexy red dress into perspective. But then her arms slid up to his hair and her fingers twined behind his neck. At her touch, he didn't want to think anymore. If she was willing, he wasn't going to reject it.

He picked her up in his arms when the elevator doors opened, carrying her into his penthouse and through to his bedroom. Gently, he stood her back on her feet, letting her body slide down the length of him, allowing both of them enjoy the friction.

His hand reached behind her and unzipped her dress, watching it pool quickly around her feet. She stood there in nothing but black, lace underwear, matching strapless bra and black, high heeled shoes.

When she tried to cover herself, he pulled her hands to rest on his hips while he reached out with one finger to trace the lace of her bra. "Are you as beautiful underneath as I imagine you will be?" he asked.

Alicia couldn't answer. By now, her hips were already moving against him in an instinctive need to feel him, to show him how much she needed him. "Please," she whispered, and reached up to push his jacket off his shoulders. The buttons on his shirt were too small and she desperately needed to touch him. In the back of her mind, she heard something rip and a part of her was horrified by the fact that she had just ripped the man's shirt but then her eyes saw his chest and she was unable to hide her fascination.

With only a slight hesitation, she reached out with her lips and tested the skin, reveling in the way his muscles shifted underneath her mouth. The sharply indrawn breath encouraged her to explore more and her mouth found the male nipple and gently reached out to tease him with her tongue.

Adam's hands gripped her arms in an effort to hold onto his control. He wanted to pull her back but let her continue at the same time. Her fascination and curiosity were driving him crazy. If everything else wasn't telling him differently, he'd swear she'd never done this before. He ignored the slight shiver in her fingers as they rested on his shoulders and enjoyed the sensual feel of her silky body against his.

"You're driving me crazy," he said, at the end of his control. He lifted her up and placed her in the center of the bed. He then stood up to take off his own clothes but was stopped in the act, stunned by how incredibly gorgeous she was. With only her skimpy black underwear covering her and sexual desire covering the rest of her, she was simply beautiful. In the past, he'd always thought women in the throes of passion were a turn on. But never before had a woman's passion affected him to the point of motionlessness.

"Please, Adam," she whispered.

Those two words broke him out of his trance and encouraged action. He swiftly pulled off his slacks and boxers, uncaring of where they landed as he lay down naked beside her. With his mouth, he kissed her lips, her neck, moving slowly down to her shoulders while his hands caressed, skimmed down her hip, her thigh, her knee, then back up the inside of her thigh. His fingers found the core of her and he was almost undone by the heat and wetness he could feel through the black lace.

"You're hot for me," he groaned. His mouth found her nipple at the same time his fingers slid inside her panties, finding her core.

The double assault on Alicia's senses and body was almost too much for her. She screamed out, her hand grabbing his wrist as her back arched off the bed.

She was mindless, unaware of what she was doing, only knowing that she had to make him understand what he was making her feel. As his head bent to take the other nipple in his mouth, her fingers slid through his hair, pulling at the soft strands and her mind reeled as his fingers continued to explore her body, reaching through the soft folds to her center.

"Adam, I can't...." she cried out as her first orgasm took over her body. "Adam!" she screamed, her body closing around his in ecstasy unimagined.

Floating down from as if on a cloud, Alicia tried to still her breathing, tried to stop the racing of her heart. But as soon as she opened her eyes, she saw the flames still evident in Adam's eyes. Her hands went to his cheeks and she kissed him softly at first, then with all the wonder she was feeling.

The kiss started the fire again and she whimpered helplessly as he took her breast with his strong hand, his fingers tweaking the nipple and his knee coming between her thighs. "I want you Alicia. Now!" he growled and took her mouth with his in a demanding kiss.

Alicia held on, unable to stop as he ripped open a package and slid the condom on. "Say you want me," he demanded.

"I do!" she cried out, her hands reaching out to touch his chest and his muscular arms. "Please," she urged, moving restlessly underneath him.

In one powerful thrust, Adam entered her, feeling the slight resistance. If he hadn't been watching her face and noticed the moment of penetration, he would have missed her reaction to him taking her virginity. But he was watching and he did notice and he was shocked by the fact.

"Alicia?" he asked, his voice hoarse as he tried to control the rampaging desire storming through his body. But her tight sheath and the slight movement of her hips as she tried to start moving again was his undoing. He tried to be gentle, knowing this was her first time but she wouldn't let him. Her movements were restless and demanding as she met him thrust for thrust and in the end, he took her over the edge to her second orgasm only moments before he found his own fulfillment.

Collapsing down on top of her, he tried to catch his ragged breath. His face was buried in her neck and her arms held him tightly around his shoulders.

A long time later, he lifted himself up onto his elbows. Pushing her hair out of her face, he stared down at her features, noting the satisfied smile and the dreamy look in her eyes.

"Alicia?" he asked, rubbing his thumb along her lower lip.

"Yes?" she replied, her tongue slipping out to touch his thumb, her fingers trailing over his shoulders.

"Are you okay?"

Her only response was to laugh and nod her head.

"Why didn't you tell me?"

She was quiet for a long moment before she looked at him. Was he mad at her?

"It didn't come up in the conversation," she said simply. Her hands wandered over his skin, reveling in the muscles that shifted wherever she touched. The reaction fascinated her and she tried it in other places, loving the way she could make his body react, just like he could do to her.

"Alicia, stop," he said and raised her hands over her head. "Why didn't you tell me you were a virgin?" he asked, his dark, intense eyes looking into her blue ones.

"What would you have done if you'd known?" she asked, looking up at him as her body felt his skin along her length.

"I damn certain wouldn't have done this," he growled.

"That's why I didn't tell you," she said, raising one leg to brush along the side of his hip.

"Alicia," he said warningly. "You can't touch me like that," he groaned, one leg capturing both of hers and trapping them so she was unable to entice him that way.

"Why?" she asked, moving her hips underneath his, feeling his body harden and come alive.

"Because you're probably too sore to deal with the consequences," he said but his mouth dropped to bite her shoulder, then sooth the area with his tongue.

Alicia gasped with the pain and pleasure his playfulness invoked. "I don't really feel very sore," she whispered. "Why don't you let go of my hands and I'll show you."

"No," he said and moved more slowly down to her breast. "I'll do it better this time."

19

Alicia stopped thinking again, her body instantly reacting to his touch and her core melting once more as his lips took her nipple in his mouth, the peak hardening instantly. "I don't think I could survive anything better," she muttered through clenched teeth but her back arched up to give him better access.

Adam chuckled but wouldn't let go of her hands. "This time, we take it slowly," he said and moved one hand down to touch her waist, his fingers circling her stomach and causing havoc with her insides.

"Slowly?" she asked, wishing he would hurry up. "Please don't on my account," she said, moving her hips, her back and writhing underneath him as the feelings his hands and mouth were creating inside her drove her to the brink of insanity. "Adam, please let me go. I want to touch you too," she said.

He looked into her eyes. "Fine. The second time is usually a little slower for a man anyway," he said and released her hands.

As soon as her hands were free she moved them over his back, her legs wrapping around his waist and her body showing him how much she wanted him. Her mouth touched his shoulder and repeated his ministration and Alicia was thrilled when he clenched his teeth as well. "Alicia, you've got to stop," he said and rolled her on top of him.

Alicia stared down at him, her eyes confused but her body thoroughly enjoying the new position. She was sitting on his muscular stomach, her hands free to touch, to feel and her eyes could see much more from this vantage point.

"Adam?" she said, her voice asking the question her thoughts couldn't form and her eyes showing him her confusion and questions.

He took charge by placing her hands on his chest while his moved up her thighs, then inside to tease her swollen flesh. "No," she whispered. "I want to..."

She didn't finish her sentence but her body bent so her lips could kiss, taste and nibble on his chest, his nipples and lower.

"Alicia, I can't," he said when her mouth moved lower to his flat stomach. But he couldn't speak as her sexy tongue darted out, making him crazy with those little touches.

"No more," he said and rolled her back onto her back. His fingers found her heat and he was almost mindless when he found the wetness there. She was ready for him again. But he still took more time, watching in fascination as her body clenched around his fingers, her mouth fell open and her fingernails ran down his arms.

"Adam, no more, please. I can't take anymore," she cried and a tear slipped out from her eye.

"You're so responsive," he groaned and quickly put on protection, then entered her as slowly as his aching body would let him. He tried to enter her slowly, inch by inch, making sure she really was ready for him but she wouldn't let him go gradually. When he wouldn't give her what her body needed, she lifted her hips and pulled him inside her, throwing her head back as he embedded himself fully inside her warmth.

"You're beautiful," he groaned and that was the last coherent thought he had as her body moved restlessly underneath him and he was unable to hold back, his whole being bent on possessing this slender siren who seemed to command his body.

After only a few strokes, Alicia cried out her release, the sensations rocking her body were more intense than before and almost never ending as he pounded into her. She came one more time before he finally found his own release, then collapsed against her. This time, he had just enough energy to roll off of her, but he pulled her next to him, cradling her head on his shoulder, one hand playing with the hair that was coming down all around her shoulders.

Adam continued to stroke her soft skin while staring at the ceiling, trying to make sense out of the evening. But after several minutes of listening to her sighs, feeling her smile against his shoulder and her soft hands on his stomach, he stopped thinking and just enjoyed the most sexually compatible woman he'd ever met.

"Shower," he said and stood up. Then he bent down and lifted her into his arms, carrying her into a large, white and black marble bathroom. The room was larger than her entire apartment she thought but was even more amazed when he opened a glass door to a shower room that had three shower heads on it. He lowered her to the floor and reached behind her to turn on the water. Instantly, warm water was flowing over her sensitized skin. Alicia had been bracing for cold water, knowing that in her apartment, it took almost fifteen minutes of running the water before any sort of heat reached her shower.

"This is wonderful," she said and turned her face into the spray.

Adam pulled the pins out of her hair, massaging the scalp as he released each tangled pin. "You have beautiful hair. You shouldn't ever wear it pinned up like this," he said, gently wrapping his hand in her hair and pulling her head back for his kiss.

Instantly, she wrapped her arms around his shoulders but she was too lethargic, her body too satisfied. Until his hands settled on her bottom. She was leaning against his body as he slowly soaped her back and arms. She tried to hide her body's reaction, thinking he would assume she was a wanton but when her muscles tensed as he touched her thighs, he laughed.

"Alicia, you can't hide your reaction. Why are you trying?" he asked, lifting her head up with his hand to kiss her again.

"I don't understand what you do to me," she said, her eyes confused but still glazed over with desire.

He pulled her hand towards him and encouraged her to touch his own body. "Why try?" he asked. "Just enjoy it," he said, his voice husky and his eyes closed as her fingers wrapped around his hardness.

Spinning her around so she was under the spray, he rinsed them off quickly. "Shower is done," he said and whipped a towel around her. With infinite slowness, he dried her legs, his mouth kissing each part that was dried. As soon as he was done, he carried her back to his bed, rolled on protection, entered her and took them back to the pinnacle of satisfaction, then over the edge again, his mouth absorbing her gasp of satisfaction as he too found his release.

Chapter 3

Alicia awoke the next morning to dim sunlight streaming through the windows. The previous night slowly came back to her and her face turned red, embarrassment growing in the light of day.

She turned slowly to see if he was still there, but she shouldn't have wondered. As soon as she moved, his arm, which had been lying over her waist, tightened their hold and pulled her against his chest.

Alicia bit her lip as her body instantly reacted yet again to their nakedness. They had made love so many times during the night, she had lost count a few hours ago. She suspected that she'd had less than two hours of sleep the whole night and, if he woke up, she knew that their marathon would continue.

Maggie! Alicia remembered that she and her sister were supposed to go out for breakfast. The bedside clock showed that it was just a little past seven o'clock in the morning and she breathed a sigh of relief. Her sister was a late sleeper, loving to pass the morning away until at least nine o'clock whenever possible.

Moving carefully, she inched her way out of the bed, praying that he wouldn't wake up and touch her again. She knew exactly where that would lead to and she was too embarrassed by her actions of the night before to see his reaction in the morning.

Alicia didn't know how she achieved it, but she finally tiptoed out of the room, her clothes in her hands. She dressed quickly in the hallway, then wandered down in search of the door. She hadn't noticed anything last night when he'd taken her here but it only took two wrong turns before she found the front door. There was an elaborate security system on the panel but she was able to step out of the penthouse with only a little bit of trouble. The elevator was another trick since it required a code to move. But she finally found the phone and reached the security guard in the lobby who started the elevator from some sort of command post.

Alicia smiled gratefully to the man as she walked by, incredibly embarrassed to be seen walking through the lobby of a very expensive building in an evening gown so early in the morning. But the man only smiled professionally at her and tipped his hat as she walked out onto the street.

Luckily, she was able to catch a cab almost immediately and was back in her apartment twenty minutes later. She closed the door quietly, noting that her sister was still curled up on the sofa, a blanket pulled over her shoulders as she slept peacefully.

Alicia went into her room and pulled off the dress, hanging it carefully in the closet then turning to the shower. The water took only ten minutes this morning but the warm water, when it finally did come, served to remind her of the shower she and Adam had shared only hours ago. Her body wanted him again and he wasn't even here. Just her memories.

Sighing, Alicia crawled into bed and pulled the covers up, intending to get a few hours of sleep before her sister woke up. But she could only stare out the window as the sun rose over the gray buildings of New York City and her body remembered every aching detail of the night before.

Chapter 4

A month later, Alicia walked into her office at Global Industries and sat down, sighing as she noted the stack of audits that were still piled up on her desk. She loved her job, but lately, she had been hard pressed to concentrate. Almost daily, she found herself staring off into space remembering her one night of passion with the most exciting man of her dreams. Or when she was walking down the street, she searched the faces of each person, wondering if she would ever run into Adam again.

She didn't even know his last name! What would her mother or sister think if they ever found out what a wanton person she had turned into that night?

If she had any sense, she would find the man and throw herself at him once again. The blush on her face at the idea was, thankfully, not witnessed by any of her co-workers since she was usually the first person into the office each morning.

Taking the first file off the top of her in-box, she forced her mind to concentrate on her work. If she didn't pick up the speed, she was going to get a stern talking to by her supervisor who had been throwing concerned looks her way for the past couple of weeks.

She liked and respected Nancy who had taken her in several months ago when she'd been looking for a job that paid more. Because of Nancy's generosity with Alicia's starting salary, Alicia had been able to pay off her mother's mortgage much more quickly than anticipated. Which was now how she found herself in her current position of working only one job for the first time in more than ten years.

Two hours later, Alicia had managed to get through a large portion of the morning's work when her supervisor stuck her head in. "How in the world do you know Adam Meyers?" Nancy Peterson asked, sitting down in the chair in front of Alicia's desk with a surprised expression on her face.

Nancy laughed at Alicia's stunned expression. "I can see by the look on your face that you know of the man in question."

Alicia thought frantically. How in the world could Nancy know Adam? They definitely didn't run in the same circles. "Yes, I met him at the spring ball last month. At least I think it was Adam Meyers. I don't know his last name," she explained. When Nancy looked at her curiously, waiting for more of an explanation, Alicia went on to say, "We didn't really get to the last name phase before I had to leave." None of that was a lie but the un-told truth behind her statement caused her to blush.

Nancy looked suspiciously at Alicia, her brows coming together, "Are we talking about the same man; tall, gorgeous, black hair, incredibly sexy eyes and a body to die for?"

Alicia licked her lips, remembering touching and tasting the body Nancy was discussing. She looked down at her papers, hiding her instantaneous reaction to the description of the man she now thought of as her "dream man". "Yes, that sounds like we're talking about the same man. What about him?"

Nancy laughed, completely thrilled with her bombshell. "Well, lucky you! But now he wants to see you in his office. Immediately."

"His office?" she asked, knowing that her mouth was hanging open but unable to do anything about it but look on as if the world and everything in it had just turned purple.

Nancy nodded her head vigorously, her eyes alight with glee and a small amount of jealousy. "Of course. Top floor."

Alicia's pencil dropped from her numb fingers but she ignored the small clatter. Nothing was getting through to her consciousness but the words that were being spoken by her boss. "Are you saying that Adam...Adam Meyers...works here?" Alicia was almost afraid to hear

26

the answer. Her whole body tight with anticipation.

Nancy's mouth fell open. "Are you kidding?" At Alicia's blank stare and negative nod, she continued. "You could say that he works here. He owns the whole company." She chuckled at Alicia's horrified expression. "Correction, he owns a majority of the stock, I should say," she corrected herself. "The man literally built this company from nothing. He's the mastermind behind our exponential growth over the past several years."

Alicia's mind refused to accept this information. "He owns the company?" she asked weakly, her stomach actually turning slightly sick at this latest news.

Nancy nodded vigorously. "Sure! How could you not know that? Everyone knows about Adam Meyers. Good grief, he's on the nightly news or in the newspapers almost weekly at times, depending on what new acquisition he's buying into. In fact, more than half the female staff watch the nightly news or read the newspapers solely for a glance at that man, he's so gorgeous," she gushed, rolling her eyes and pretending to shiver in delight then fan herself as if she were overheated.

Alicia closed her mouth and breathed a sigh of relief. She felt almost silly for assuming that Nancy was talking about the man who had occupied her mind almost constantly in the past month, both day and night. "We must be thinking of different people," Alicia said, shaking her head. "The Adam I know is only in his mid-thirties."

Nancy grinned with unabashed enthusiasm. "Yep, that's the one. Like I said; tall, incredibly gorgeous with black hair, great body..." Nancy sighed in happiness just thinking about him. "Is that the man you met?"

Alicia could only nod her head. She didn't add that she'd spent one, incredible night with him, ravaging his body, allowing him to do things to hers that she couldn't ever repeat and then slinking out of his apartment like a dockside hussy the following morning. Even now, she was ashamed of how she'd acted that night.

"You probably didn't realize who he is because you never watch television and, with the three jobs you used to work, never had time to read the newspapers. Well, you'd better hurry. The illustrious man is waiting for you in his office." Nancy announced that little tid bit and started to get up out of the chair she'd been occupying for the past few minutes.

Alicia gripped the side of her desk, her knuckles turning white with Nancy's words. "Me? Why on earth would he want to see me?" she squeaked. She hoped she didn't know. How would she face him? Just thinking about the things they'd done made her face flame into color again.

"Dunno," she laughed, "but you'd better hurry." Nancy stood up and left the office, leaving Alicia to stare at the empty chair, her whole body starting to tremble with nerves and shame. And memories!

Alicia put down her pen and slowly stood up, smoothing her neat, professional navy skirt as she walked. In the elevator, she pressed the button for the top floor and looked down at her outfit, wondering if she looked too dowdy. Her hair was pulled back into a tight chignon at the nape of her neck and her slim navy skirt ended just above her knees. She pulled the matching navy jacket down more smoothly over her stomach and gently touched the faux pearl necklace at her throat. She suspected that she looked like a school marm but that couldn't be helped, she supposed.

The elevator doors opened and she stepped out into the eerie quiet of the executive offices.

Jim Peterson, head of security, had watched Adam's reaction as he'd laid the folder open twenty minutes ago. The evidence was irrefutable against the woman. There had been other transgressions in the past against Global Corp but he'd never seen Adam react the same way. It was as if he were taking this latest investigation as a personal slap in the face. That wasn't the usual cool, calm and merciless man he'd worked with for the past ten years.

When he'd brought up the issue two weeks ago about suspected embezzlement, Jim hadn't had any idea who was doing the work. It had taken long hours of tracing information back to the source, often off in the wrong direction, only to backtrack to his starting point again before he finally narrowed the data to the female mentioned in the file. He also had a picture of her, taken when she'd posed for her security badge. She was definitely a beauty, he thought. And her image came across as innocent looking. But in his experience, looks rarely played a factor in guilt or innocence.

"I could be wrong," Jim mentioned but the man staring out the window didn't move.

"Do you really doubt your findings?" Adam asked briskly without turning around.

Jim thought about the small, niggling details he hadn't been able to figure out yet, but shook his head. He'd eventually resolve them as well but the case was pretty concrete as it was now. "Not really. There's always some doubt," he explained. "But the facts in this case lend themselves to a pretty solid case."

A moment later, a petite and stunningly beautiful woman in a conservative but fashionable navy blue suit stepped into the doorway. "I was told to come up to your office," Alicia said hesitantly. "I'm sorry but your secretary isn't at her desk or I would have waited."

Jim was curious about the blush that stole into her cheeks and the look in her eyes. It was not what he was expecting. In fact, she was so attuned to Adam, she didn't even realize that Jim was also in the room.

Adam turned and looked the woman up and down, his eyes hard and his features completely blank. "So we meet again," he said softly.

Alicia wished she could just ease back down to the safety of her office but she tried to put on a brave, sophisticated front. "So it would seem," she said and smiled briefly, her eyes glancing down to the carpet.

Adam watched her perfectly porcelain skin turn a becoming shade of pink and gritted his teeth. What an actress, he thought. But no more! He'd spent too many hours trying to find this woman. So having her appear back in his life in this way, as a criminal, made him doubt all of his recollections of their one night together.

Pushing those thoughts aside, he crossed his arms over his chest and surveyed her petite form for a long moment. "Please come in and have a seat," Adam snapped. "Let me introduce you to Jim Peterson. He's the head of security for Global Industries."

Alicia walked into the room and smiled graciously at the man, shaking his hand before she took the seat opposite Adam's desk.

Adam continued to stand, an intimidating, forceful persona that seemed to emanate anger and hostility. "Now that the pleasantries are over with, perhaps you could explain this to me," Adam said and pushed the file with all the evidence across his desk. It stopped at the edge and Alicia reached out to take the file, the only expression on her face was one of professional curiosity.

Jim watched intently as the woman calmly opened the file and searched through the documents. She shook her head several times. "I'm sorry, this isn't right," she said as she ran a tapered fingernail down several checks that had been made out to a dummy bank account. She turned the page and shook her head again, her brow furrowed in confusion. "This isn't protocol either," she said and glanced up at Adam. "The accounting rules don't allow this to happen," she said but kept flipping through the documents.

Adam put his hands on his hips and waited impatiently until she got past all the checks for large amounts. The evidence that convicted her was after the checks. It showed her name as the beneficiary of all the dummy accounts with her own signature at the bottom. There were also several pages of her signature that had witnesses to it, as well as the security signature that compared her signature to the dummy accounts in case they were different.

He knew the exact moment she realized she'd been caught. Her finger stopped moving along the document, right at her signature. "This isn't right!" she said, gasping but her hands continued to sift through the following pages.

She saw her own picture and directly behind that, the most damning evidence possible, at least in his own mind. It was an article about her father that described his conviction for embezzlement ten years ago and how he'd subsequently been killed in a prison fight. By the time she picked up the article, her fingers were trembling. Her eyes went to Adam and she was already shaking her head. "It isn't true," she said forcefully. "I didn't steal this money."

"Isn't that what all thieves say?" Adam asked sarcastically, sneering with contempt at her act of innocence in the face of overwhelming evidence.

Her fingers clutched the papers to her lap and she looked up imploringly to Adam. "You have to believe me. Yes, my father embezzled money from the company he worked for but I know what effect it had on my family. I would never jeopardize them in this way."

Jim stood up and cleared his throat. "Should I make the call?" he asked Adam.

Alicia had forgotten his presence in the room but she turned to him now, willing the older man to believe her. "I didn't steal this money! I promise," she emphatically asserted.

"I believe that's for a jury to determine," Jim replied softly but firmly. He was trying to be hard line about the situation, but there was something in her expression and the way she reacted to the initial documents that was bothering him. He couldn't quite put his finger on it.

Adam stared at Alicia, his features tight against his bone structure. He was watching her, his jaw clenched as she read through the evidence against her once more.

Adam finally acknowledged Jim's question after coming to a conclusion himself. "No. I'll take it from here," he said brusquely to the other man, not bothering to look his way as he continued to watch Alicia with a steely glare. "I'll call you if I need you."

Alicia was having a hard time breathing as she watched the older man leave the office. The soft click of the door as he left sounded like the snap of a prison door. She was in a panic. Even the smallest accusations like this would destroy her mother who hung on to reality with only a fine thread of sanity. And Maggie! Her career would be ruined. She'd only been working in her current job for two months. A senator would never be able to keep the sister of a criminal, even a suspected one, on his staff.

Lifting her tear brightened eyes to Adam, she implored him, "You have to believe me! I promise you, I had nothing to do with this."

"All evidence to the contrary," he snapped and walked around to the front of his desk to look down at her. He was furious, both with himself and with her. He'd been searching for this woman ever since he'd

31

woken up after their one night together and hadn't been able to find her anywhere. He'd even hired a private investigator but stopped the search after a week, feeling ridiculous that he was obsessing over a woman who obviously didn't want to be found. And then he found out that, not only was she working in the same building, drawing a salary from him but that she was stealing hundreds of thousands of dollars from him.

To make matters worse, the moment she'd walked into his office, all he'd wanted to do was to make love to her again. His body was instantly aware of every move of hers, achingly ready to sink his own body deeply into her and hear her cries of satisfaction, just as he had that one night.

At the same time, he wanted to take her into his arms and comfort her, assure her that everything would be fine.

But everything wasn't going to be fine. He was furious that this tiny woman had broken a trust twice. Once by sneaking out without a goodbye and then by stealing money from his company. He refused to admit that he was hurt by her lack of goodbye but more than willing to put an emotion on her theft. He was furious.

No one took advantage of Adam Meyers!

Walking forward, he smelled her subtle perfume and gritted his teeth. "What are you going to do about this situation?" he demanded, walking behind her and leaning down, his arms hooking onto the back of her chair and his head only inches from hers.

"Do?"

"Yes, my dear. You stole a significant amount of money from me. I want it back," he said quietly, his mouth close to her ear.

"But I didn't steal anything from you," she said breathlessly. Alicia frantically tried to come up with some way to counter all the evidence against her. Unfortunately, it was a very good case. She had no idea how her signature had gotten onto those deposit accounts but there must be some way she could prove it to him.

"Then prove it," he said.

She bit her lip, trying to come up with a response. "I can't right at the moment. But I promise I'll find out who did," she said.

"How are you going to do that?"

She pressed her body into the seat of the chair, pushing her mind to come up with a solution, one that wouldn't damn her in the process. "I'm a good auditor. I've only been working here for a few months but I have worked as an auditor since college and I'll find your money and who took it."

"That's going to be a little difficult," he said and walked around to face her, leaning against his desk in a deceptively casual stance. "Technically, you no longer work here."

Alicia gasped and spun around in her chair, "No!" Her eyes were pleading with him to not take that course of action.

Adam ignored her eyes and turned away to walk back around his desk. "Yes. I'm sorry, my dear, but I can't have a suspected embezzler continue to work for me." He watched her face drain of what color was left. Again he had to fight the urge to comfort her. He reminded himself that he only wanted her luscious, sexy body and not her mind. There was no reason to comfort her. An idea slowly formed in his mind and he liked the thought.

Alicia held her hands out in front of her, imploring him to believe her. "But I can prove it wasn't me if you'll just give me a chance!" Her panic was so acute now, she was almost physically ill. She forced her stomach to calm down in an effort to convince him that she wasn't what he thought her to be.

Crossing his arms over his chest he shrugged his shoulder. "Normally in situations like this, the culprit is just turned over to the authorities and they deal with the issue. But I'll make a deal with you. Pay back the money and I'll forget all about this, due to our short, previous relationship."

Alicia shook her head helplessly. "I don't have that kind of money." She'd never had any money. It had always gone to her sister's college expenses or her mother's mortgage and living expenses. A savings account had never even been an option until recently.

ELIZABETH LENNOX

The trap closed with her words. He felt a deep sense of satisfaction, knowing that he had her exactly where his body wanted her. After a long month where he had searched for her, failed to find her, and because of her absence, had been celibate since no other woman had even remotely interested him, he was finally obtaining retribution and satisfaction. The smile that came to his face didn't reach his eyes. They were filled with pleasure though. "Well, then, we'll have to work out a deal. Won't we?"

The look in his eyes terrified her almost as much as the thought of jail did. It wasn't a kind or concerned look. It was one of triumph.

"A deal?" she whispered, terrified of his next words and what they might mean to her future.

He walked back around to the front of her chair and pulled the file out of her hands. Placing the file behind him, he turned back and then pulled her out of the chair, right into his arms. One hand stroked her cheek as his eyes bore into hers. "Yes, a deal."

"What kind of deal?" she asked, her body already betraying her fear as his fingers touched her skin, making her body tremble at his simple touch. She tried to pull back slightly but his arms were bands of steel around her waist.

"How about a month for every ten thousand dollars you stole?"

"A month?" She tried to focus but her mind wasn't working properly. Not with his hands on her skin and around her waist.

"Yes. A month where you work for me, but in an entirely different capacity."

Alicia didn't like the way he was looking at her but she was unable to pull out of his arms. Her body felt magnetized to his and her skin was already aching for more of his touch.

"What sort of capacity?" she whispered.

His eyes sharpened and Alicia instantly knew that she wasn't going to like his explanation. "I need a mistress. And I think....no, I

34

know," he corrected, "you'd suit me quite admirably."

The idea shook her to the core. She pulled out of his arms and shook her head. "No!"

"What's wrong with becoming my mistress?" he asked, his mouth smiling as he looked downward, noting that her nipples were already hard and pressing against the fabric of her summer blouse. "I think you'd be ideally suited for the role."

Alicia was so taken aback, she almost slapped him. "I'm not a whore!" she said, her fists clenching at her sides.

He jerked at her harsh words. "No, just a criminal who has stolen a great deal of money from me," he fired back. He stepped away from her and came around the other side of his desk. "So what's your decision? Prison? Or my home?"

Chapter 5

Alicia stared at the man she'd remembered as kind and gentle. Her shuddering horror was like a physical blow and she tried to think. However, the two choices he'd offered were beyond her ability to grasp. "What do you mean your home?"

He smiled but it was more wolfish than joyful. His eyes moved down her body, surveying her slim figure. "My dear, that one night with you only whetted my appetite. I'm afraid I'm going to have a great deal of need for you." His eyes were soft for a brief moment. Then he recalled himself and straightened. "Make your decision. I don't have a lot of time at the moment," he said and glanced at his watch.

She still didn't understand completely what he was telling her. The words all connected together into a complete sentence but the meaning was too outrageous for her to absorb. Her hands went to her head, holding the sides as she tried to figure out what he was saying to her. The accusations of embezzlement were mind-boggling. And the insulting proposition was only minimally as bad.

"I'd have to live with you?" she asked, clarifying his intentions in her mind.

He raised an eyebrow, staring at her with only a slight bit of humor on his handsome face. "Of course. I want your delectable body. And I want it on demand whenever the mood strikes me."

Her mind recoiled in horror. "That's obscene," she gasped, taking another step backwards, her blue eyes looking into his hard, dark ones as if she could somehow convince him of her innocence.

His eyebrows snapped together angrily and his mouth thinned before he replied, "No, stealing that much money from me is obscene. What on earth would you need all that money for? You make a good living on what I pay you." He stood up and looked down at her dispassionately. "But then you've had your mother and sister to take care of for the past ten years, haven't you? I guess you wanted a little spoiling yourself, huh?"

Alicia's eyes widened with fear that he knew about her family.

He chuckled at her response. He walked back to her, his finger sliding down her cheek in a soft caress. "Yes, Alicia. I know all about your family and your extra jobs." He sighed heavily and the anger suddenly disappeared from his eyes. He now looked at her gently, as if he... understood? "Take the deal. I can be a very generous lover," he told her, his eyes drilling into hers. "If you want to be pampered, there's no other man who can do it as well as I can," he said.

His offer...he was gentler now, but everything about his suggestion felt wrong. "This isn't right," she said, her voice faltering as he moved closer.

"What's not right?" he asked, his hand sliding up her arm. "Our bodies were made for each other. That one night together proved that beyond any doubt in my mind. What couldn't be more right?"

What was she supposed to say? That she wanted more from a relationship than just sex? That she'd spent the last ten years taking care of two other people and wanted to experience love? The hard look in his eyes told her he wasn't interested in that. And her body was telling her that it wasn't interested in that either.

"No, I can't do it," she said, taking a deep breath and shaking her head.

Adam stepped backwards instantly, the gentleness gone from his eyes and walked around to his desk. "Fine. The police will be here in a few minutes," he said and started pressing numbers on the keypad.

"No!" she said and slammed her fingers down on the phone,

breaking the connection. "Fine!" she said in a panic. "Whatever you want."

She had no intention of following through on his proposition but needed time to figure out how to convince him of her innocence. He was angry now. She could feel the fury pulsating through his body as well as something more, something more primitive. Somehow, she had to get through to him but acceptance was the only way she could give herself additional time.

And she had to protect her sister and mother! Maggie would be fired at the first hint of scandal! And her mother...? No, her mother would never survive another arrest and trial. She was barely aware of the world now!

"I'll do it," she confirmed again, her heart aching with those words.

Adam didn't know that he would feel this victorious but the tense knot in his stomach quickly eased at her words. "Wise choice. I'll call my driver and will have him drive you to your apartment to pack some clothes. He'll then drive you to my place. I'll meet you there for dinner," he said and without another word, he pulled her closer and kissed her. It was a seal of ownership and despite Alicia's anger over his claim, her body reacted, arching into his and glorying in the hard, male strength of him.

After several minutes, when she was clinging to him and almost delirious with desire, he pulled away and stepped backwards. If she hadn't grabbed the side of his desk, she probably would have fallen to the floor.

"I see you're stepping into the agreement with finesse." His eyes raked down her body, noting her heavy breathing with satisfaction. "That's good. I'll see you at my place around seven o'clock tonight," he said. Without another word, he lifted the receiver and pressed a button. "Bill, I'm sending Alicia Miller down to you. Take her to her apartment and help her pack up her bags, then bring her to my place. Come back to get me at the usual time," he said and hung up the phone without any other comment.

"I have to get my purse," Alicia said, her hands fisted at her sides in anger and fear.

His eyes showed no mercy. "You have three minutes to get downstairs. If you don't meet Bill at the front entrance, I'll assume you're trying to escape and will call the police, shutting down the building so you can't get away," he told her curtly.

Alicia didn't look at him but she nodded her head. Without another word, she rushed out of the office and almost ran down the hallway to the elevator.

By the time she reached the lobby, she was breathless and knew she was about to run out of time. It was an awful feeling to be so controlled by another human being but she rationalized that she'd never really had any freedom. From the moment her father started embezzling money all those years ago, her life's die had been cast. Oh, she could have gone about her happy way and finished high school in a foster home, separated from her sister while her mother would be institutionalized. But her upbringing, minus the criminal her father had been, wouldn't let her do that to her family.

And now she was again trapped, taking care of her sister's career and her mother's delicate mental state against the horrible accusations that had been thrown at her this morning. As she watched the buildings pass in a blur through the limousine window, she thought back to her morning and how she'd been so thrilled with her one memory of her crazy evening with the man of her dreams.

Alicia laughed harshly, ignoring the startled look from the driver through the rear view mirror. She'd never even had a boyfriend. From the time she could start dating and was interested in boys, she'd had to start working. Initially to put food on the table as her mother attended the trial of her father. And then, after their savings ran out, she'd had to work another job just to keep the house.

Between several jobs
and either high school or college, she'd never had any spare time but hadn't minded, knowing that her sister was doing extremely well in school and her mother was still at home to help them, although not emotionally capable of helping herself.

And now, she was going to be imprisoned again. Not by iron bars or by crushing financial burdens but by a man who had no feelings for her other than anger and sex. It was humiliating but she bit her finger to distract herself from crying. She would wait until she was alone before she broke down in tears.

At this time of the morning, it took less than twenty minutes before the limousine was pulling up in front of her apartment building. The worn, dilapidated exterior was indicative of the poor interior. But it was cheap and conveniently located close to her job which was all she'd needed while she paid off debts and expenses.

Alone in her apartment, she looked around. There wasn't much to pack. In an effort to put more money towards her sister's college expenses or her mother's mortgage, she rarely spent money on herself. She had five work suits for the summer and five for the winter months. She had a few pairs of jeans and shorts. All her furniture was of the garage sale quality and she didn't own a television since she rarely had time to relax and watch it.

She only packed her clothes, feeling a little desperate and not really sure what he'd meant by her being his mistress. He'd said as much, but surely he didn't want her to live with him, did he? That was a little drastic for only a one night acquaintance. Maybe he was just angry and would calm down once he'd had more time to think about the situation and the potential ramifications of having someone live with him that he didn't really know.

Working that through in her mind, she felt slightly better but still ashamed that she was packing a small bag with a spare set of clothes regardless, she locked the door behind her and went down the five flights of stairs to the street level where Adam's driver was still waiting for her. Instead of packing all of her clothes, she left everything but her two best suits, her shorts and a pair of jeans, leaving the rest in her apartment.

When she exited her apartment building, Bill was standing beside the limousine and immediately opened the car door for her. "Thank you," she said and ducked her head inside.

He drove her through the streets and back along the road that was familiar only because she remembered the morning ride away from it. Adam's apartment building was completely different from her own.

In her building, Alicia picked up her mail in the lobby and sometimes off the floor as things spilled out from the open spaces of her mail cubby. The lobby of her building was of whitewashed cement and linoleum flooring, cracking in the corners and with light bulbs that usually didn't work. Adam's building was magnificently decorated with marble and brass, lovely trees situated in strategic places and soft music playing discreetly in the background.

The security guard, who had obviously been informed of her imminent arrival, tipped his hat to her and provided her with the code to reach Adam's penthouse apartment through the private elevator. She smiled gratefully to him but was too embarrassed by her predicament to be completely open with him.

Bill dropped her bag down in the entry way and then immediately bowed out of the apartment. Alicia was left alone, just standing in the middle of the large foyer wondering what she was supposed to do now. It was only four o'clock in the afternoon and she was completely lost, unable to figure out how to deal with her current situation and scared to death.

Taking a deep breath, she supposed that she should explore Adam's place a little more. But just being here made her feel as if the world was wrong and she was tipping sideways, isolated and punished for something she didn't do.

Chapter 6

Adam strode into the penthouse at seven-thirty that night. He eagerly looked around for Alicia, ready to christen their agreement and see if they were really as good as he remembered or if it was only in his imagination.

He noticed her bag by the door and walked into the living room. She wasn't there. He checked in the office but still, no one was waiting for him. He was about to become angry when he heard the small noise coming from somewhere in the kitchen area. It was a place that he knew existed but he rarely stepped into. He had a cook that left him meals he heated up, but most of the time, he had social obligations that kept him out in the evenings. Caterers used the kitchen more often than he did so it was not the first place he would think to look.

But there she was, sitting sadly at the counter with a plate in front of her with a lone sandwich, uneaten.

Adam hardened his heart against her pitiful state. He reminded himself of all the evidence against her and his feelings that morning a month ago when he'd woken up, reached out for her but only encountered empty space. He'd been furious that morning but even more so after a week of searching for her with no luck.

Adam tossed those feelings aside as being useless. He had her right where he wanted her and wasn't about to let her go just because she was a good actress.

"What's for dinner?" he asked, walking briskly into the kitchen.

Alicia jumped almost a foot, then put a hand to her throat, trying to calm down her racing heart. But it was useless as her eyes followed him across the kitchen. He was incredibly virile and overwhelmingly male, she thought as she watched him loosen his tie, staring at her the whole time.

"Anything good?" he asked, and peered down at her uneaten sandwich. "Hmm, not really," he said, then looked back at her. "But in fact, I'm not very hungry for food," he said.

Alicia understood exactly what he was trying to tell her and her mind rebelled against the idea of just falling into bed with him again. They had to talk and somehow she had to make him understand that she wasn't that kind of person.

"Adam, that night... a month ago..." she stopped, unsure of how to proceed.

"Yes?" he asked, one eyebrow raised as he took a bite of her sandwich, watching her with his dark, intense eyes the whole time.

She fiddled with the practical watch on her wrist, unable to look at the achingly handsome and dynamic man who was staring down at her, thinking of her as a criminal. "It wasn't really me."

Adam smiled for the first time that day. "I'd like you to explain who exactly it was," he chuckled. "I was there too and I distinctly remember you being a very active participant."

She flushed at his amusement and looked down at her hands that were fluttering around in her nervousness. "Well, yes. But that wasn't like me. I don't go around having one night stands."

"That night wouldn't have been one if you'd not slipped out like some sort of..."

She wouldn't let him finish but put her hand over his mouth to cover it up, barring him from saying whatever he was going to say. "I'm not like that. I'd never slept with anyone before."

He pulled her hand away from his mouth, his lips brushing the inside of her wrist "I don't remember there being a lot of sleeping going on that night either."

Alicia pursed her lips in frustration. "You know what I'm trying to say," she shot back then stood up angrily, crossing her arms over her stomach as if the action would ward off the pain and humiliation she was feeling. She walked around the room, wishing she was anywhere but here in this amazing penthouse with the most devastatingly handsome man she'd ever met her in life, who was looking at her as if she were a bug on his shoe.

Adam had had enough. Her pacing had only shown off her figure, not that he thought she realized it, but the view reminded him of what he wanted from her. "Yes. I know what you're trying to say and I know you weren't like that." He reached out and took her wrist in his strong hand, the grip not hurting but she couldn't break his hold even if she tried. "But now we know exactly what you are," he said softly, menacingly, "so let's just get around to what we both are thinking about. How about if we adjourn from the kitchen and into the bedroom where we can relax and enjoy each other's company more?" he said, taking her hand in his and pulling her along behind him.

Alicia tried to pull her hand away but his hold wasn't as loose, nor as gentle, as she'd thought. "Adam, you're not listening to me."

He didn't bother to stop, just kept pulling her towards the long hallway she vaguely remembered led to his bedroom. "Perhaps because you're not saying anything that interests me," he replied and stepped forward to cover her mouth with his.

Alicia tried to resist and pull her head back, but he only put a hand to the back of her head and nibbled seductively on her lower lip. The first contact was shockingly erotic and Alicia gasped, allowing his mouth full access to hers. He took advantage of her surprise and slid a hand underneath her silk shirt. Alicia gripped his shoulders, unable to stand on her own with the onslaught of passion he was able to invoke so easily. Her mind told her to fight him, to pull away but her body simply stood there, responding but still confused by the mixed messages.

"Adam, please," she said, a tear slipping out from her eye with the shame of the situation. But she wasn't sure if she was pleading with him to stop or continue.

"I know," he said and took the decision into his hands by lifting her into his arms. Just like the last time, he effortlessly swung her up and carried her into his bedroom. She had a slight moment of panic but then her arms had to slide around his neck to hold her steady and her fingers curled into his hair. The touch reminded her of how freely she had touched him everywhere that night and her body took over where her mind pulled back.

With ease, he discarded her clothes and pulled her to him, naked and throbbing. "You're just as beautiful as I remember," he said as he laid her down in the center of his bed.

Alicia melted with his sweet words and her mouth became dry as he stood over her, taking off his own clothes. She could no longer argue against the actions that were going to happen than she could stop breathing. She accepted that she wanted him desperately. Watching him undress was like nothing she'd ever imagined. Each piece of skin that he revealed made her more desperate to have his touch back against her skin.

As soon as he was free of his clothes, he came down to her, his hands searching everywhere, his mouth exploring and Alicia cried out as the feelings and sensations washed over her.

He entered her quickly, smoothly. An easy feat as her body was more than ready for him. And since her body remembered the path his had taken her the last time and had craved the touch for so many nights, she climaxed almost instantly around him, her mind reeling as the feelings ripped through her body.

That night formed the pattern for the following two weeks. Adam would come home in the evening, usually around nine or ten o'clock at night, he would immediately make love to her and they would fall asleep in each other's arms, completely replete and exhausted. Usually, he woke her up several times during the night, then in the morning with a kiss and more passion, leaving her worn out and shaking from his touch and the instantaneous way he could make her body respond.

Alicia was left alone for the rest of the day with nothing to do. She found that Sylvia, the maid, came in on Wednesdays to scrub the entire penthouse and, Gerard, the cook came in on Thursdays to make several complete meals and leave them in the refrigerator for Adam, all prepared to simply heat up and serve. She made friends with both, knowing they were the only people she could communicate with. She helped Sylvia with the scrubbing, enjoying the older woman's soft humor and gentle way of looking at life. From Gerard, she discovered that she really loved to cook. As a child, she remembered making cookies with her mother and sister, but after her father's arrest, she'd never had the time to cook, much less learn the finer points of gourmet cuisine. He would show her different tricks while they talked, forming a friendship.

In the middle of the day, she would usually walk out to the park and watch the mothers play with their children on the swing sets, jealously wondering if her life would ever be normal again. Would she ever have children? A husband? It was a depressing thought to wonder about something like that. An idea that had always been a definite at some point in the future had suddenly turned to a maybe because of her precarious position. She wasn't even sure if she'd ever be able to find another job, much less find a husband and have children with him.

She kept those thoughts to a minimum, knowing that they wouldn't do any good. She had to keep thinking positively and trying to figure out how the embezzlement had happened. But without a computer, she was limited in what she could investigate.

When she wasn't cooking, cleaning or worrying, she also got to know several of the tenants in Adam's building. Although the mail was delivered to the apartments instead of to a mail room like normal people, she walked so often, the tenants started to recognize her and say hello. She also made sure to call her sister and mother once a week so neither would worry about her. Her phone calls kept them from calling her at work where they would surely find out that she was no longer employed by Global Corporation and would start asking questions.

Alicia never brought up the reason why she was living in his apartment. Not because she didn't want to, but simply because there was no time. Adam worked hard, leaving early in the morning and not coming home until late in the evening. At that point, he simply pulled her into his arms and made love to her for the rest of the night. Alicia had tried on several occasions to speak with him, to try and get him to understand her point of view or at least claim her innocence one more time but each time she started to talk about it, Adam simply covered her mouth with his and the feelings instantly accelerated into passion instead of reason.

Alicia felt awful. She was living in limbo where her days were spent with Adam's hired help. But she couldn't really complain since that's basically what he considered her. He had a maid and chef who came in during the working hours, never having met their employer. And during the nights, she was also his, but he met her in bed, the passion always just under the surface.

The Friday afternoon of the third week, he called her and told her she needed to dress up since they had to go out. Alicia hesitated on the phone. "Adam, what exactly do you mean by 'dress up'?" she asked carefully.

"I mean, wear something fancy. I have no idea what women call them but it must be elegant and sophisticated."

Alicia bit her lip. "Adam, I don't want to go out," she lied. It wasn't that she didn't want to go out. It was more about the fact that she didn't really have anything appropriate to wear. She spent her days in jeans and shorts and her nights in nothing at all.

She could feel his anger through the phone. "I don't really care what you want. Be ready by six o'clock," he snapped and hung up the phone.

Alicia wasn't as calm. She was furious. She stormed out of the apartment and went for a long walk in the park. Should she just bend to his will? What were her alternatives? She could fight him all she wanted but the reality was, he could and probably would, immediately call the police. He had a trump card and she couldn't afford to call his bluff.

Walking back into the penthouse an hour later, she glanced at the clock. It was already four o'clock. With a deep sigh, she grabbed her purse and her apartment key, then headed over to her old apartment. She picked up the only dress that might qualify, the one she'd worn that fateful night they'd met. Looking at it now, she wanted to crush it in her hands and rip it to shreds.

On the bus ride back, she wondered if she wasn't being too harsh on the dress. After all, if she hadn't worn the dress, she'd never have met Adam and he would have seen the evidence piled up against her and simply called the police. Since they had met, he'd given her a type of reprieve, if that was an accurate way to look at the situation. She was now in his luxurious apartment and the lover of a passionate man that took her breath away.

Looking at it that way, she should actually be grateful for this dress. It had probably saved her from a lot of legal expenses not to mention public humiliation.

Back in Adam's penthouse, hooked the hangar onto the top of a door. It wasn't so bad, she told herself. Life could be a whole lot worse. That didn't stop the pang of anger that welled up inside of her though. She was still here and Adam made love to her every night but never spoke to her about anything other than mild inquiries into her day.

Taking the dress off the hanger and laying it on the bed, she accepted that she had no alternative but to wear the dress again and relive that night. She showered and changed into the red dress, no longer considering herself pretty or sexy in the color or style. She only felt cheap and used.

She couldn't create the same effect with her hair as Maggie had that night so she settled for a sleek pony tail with a sophisticated clip at her nape.

Alicia was standing in the middle of his brown and tan living room, waiting for Adam when he walked in at six o'clock that evening.

"Reminding me of something?" he asked, his eyes traveling up and down her body clad in the red silk evening gown.

Alicia blushed, wishing she could appear more sophisticated around him. "No. This is the only sophisticated dress I own," she explained. "If you don't like it, I'd be happy to change into one of my navy suits," she said, her chin going up a notch as she returned his stare.

Adam noted the challenge in her face and walked over to her, staring down into her lovely, angry features. "Ah, the lady has fire outside of the bedroom as well," he said, his knuckles coming up to her chin, rubbing gently. "I was wondering."

After all her soul searching of the afternoon, she wasn't going to take this kind of teasing tonight. Her eyes flashed fire as she said, "The lady has claws too," she said, pulling her chin away and stepping backwards. "Like I said, if you don't like it..." she left the suggestion dangling.

"Who said I didn't like it?" he asked, his eyes moving down her slender figure that was lush in all the right places. "I think it looks beautiful on you."

She was caught off guard by the compliment and confused by his gentle tone. "Th...thank you," she said, her eyes losing some of the anger almost instantly.

"You're welcome. But I'm guessing you are telling me that you need more clothes," he commented and turned away from her. "I told you I'd be generous. All you had to do was tell me," he called back to her a moment before he disappeared into his bedroom.

Alicia just stood there staring at the empty doorway. "You are the most confusing man," she said to herself.

Fifteen minutes later, Adam walked back out looking devastatingly handsome, freshly showered and shaved wearing a tailored tuxedo. "Ready?" he asked and offered his arm.

"Where are we going?" she asked, taking his arm and smiling tentatively at him.

"Dinner with a business acquaintance," was all he would say to her.

Bill was at the front door waiting for them with the limousine door open. Within moments the car was smoothly carrying them through the heavy, evening rush hour traffic with miraculous ease. They arrived at the restaurant only a few minutes later and were immediately shown to their table.

Adam introduced her to the people that were already gathered at the large table. They were foreign business people with their significant others and wives. Alicia sat next to Adam who basically ignored her throughout the entire meal. But she didn't mind. He was listening intently to some sort of business arrangement with the men next to and across from her and she was perfectly content to listen to the women next to her discuss their children. The conversation was lively and humorous as the women told funny stories of their children's antics.

When dessert arrived, the ladies excused themselves and made their way to the bathroom. Adam had already gone to another room, apparently to discuss a business issue so Alicia was left at the table for several minutes with no one to talk to. She felt incredibly alone all of a sudden and very self-conscious. She fiddled with the dessert of chocolate mousse, not really hungry at all but needing something to do with her hands and her eyes.

"Good evening," a male voice said next to her.

Alicia looked up quickly and smiled at one of the husbands of the women who had just left. "Good evening. Richard, correct?" she asked, relieved to not be all alone again. The man had kind eyes, she thought.

"You look very lonely, sitting here by yourself. Where did everyone go?"

"Your wife and Doris are in the bathroom. They should be back any moment now."

"That's good," he said. "Glad to know she hasn't deserted me. I'd hate to have to get the kids dressed in the morning. Little hellions, you know," he grimaced, taking a sip of wine.

Alicia laughed since his wife had just been talking about the morning routine in their house. "Yes, I'd heard that it can be a little chaotic."

Richard laughed harshly. "Chaotic is a nice word for what goes on. What about you?" he asked, placing his wine glass down on the table and turning to face her. "What's your story?'

Alicia was instantly wary. How did one explain that she was the unpaid mistress to a man who thinks she was a criminal? "Oh, you know, just the usual."

Richard smiled. "I can't imagine anything you do being usual. What line of work are you in?" he asked.

"I am an accountant," she said, without lying. At least, she hoped she wasn't lying. Was her license taken away? The thought made her heart skip several beats but she forced the panic aside. If that was the case, she'd deal with it later. Tonight wasn't the time or place to worry about that.

"Interesting! I studied accounting in college one semester," he said, shaking his head. "Never could understand all those debits and credits. Too much adding and subtracting. I always came up with the wrong answer."

The people slowly filtered back to the table but the ladies didn't take their old seats. As everyone shifted, Alicia found herself with Richard on one side of her and Adam on the other. Adam glared at her during the rest of her conversation with Richard, even though his wife was sitting right next to him, laughing and joking about the renovations on their kitchen and the issues surrounding the feeding of four children with no stove or refrigerator.

Once coffee was served, Adam stood up next to her. "Let's dance," he said and took Alicia's hand without waiting for a reply.

Alicia almost didn't stand up with him but the look in his eyes told her he wanted her to challenge him. She decided not to give in to him and cause a scene. But she stood stiffly in his arms as he guided her across the ballroom.

"Anger won't work, my dear," he said and pulled her closer to his body. "Nor will enticing Richard with that delectable body of yours. He doesn't have enough money anyway but he won't leave his wife for you."

"What on earth are you talking about?" she asked, trying to pull out of his arms. She understood he was accusing her of something but wasn't sure exactly what she might have done wrong in his eyes. "Richard is a very nice person and I'm completely aware that he's married."

"Yes. I'm glad you picked up on that."

Alicia rolled her eyes. "How could I not have picked up on that little piece of information when I sat next to his wife all evening?"

His anger seeped through the pleasant façade he'd been projecting. He gritted his teeth while saying, "Then you know that they are a great couple. So don't try and break them up just to save your own skin. He'd never be able to pay off your debt to me so just forget about it."

Alicia gasped, horrified at what he was implying. "Are you saying I was flirting with Richard?" she demanded, wishing he would release her hand so she could slap him.

"Weren't you?"

"Absolutely not!" she spat out at him. "They are a very nice couple and, unlike you, I take people at face value. All they talk about is their kids and I could easily tell that they are very dedicated to each other. It is nice to know there are normal couples out there that don't see the world and the people in them as simple dollars signs. You have a very warped view of the world, Adam." She looked away, not wanting him to see the hurt in her eyes caused by his accusations. Alicia couldn't believe that Adam had misinterpreted a simple, pleasant conversation as flirtation with another man.

"Just tell me you weren't thinking of having Richard replace me once we're through."

"No!" she snapped, furious with him for believing such an awful thing. "You're awful."

There was a long silence and Alicia could feel his eyes looking at her features but she refused to look at him. She pretended to watch the other dancers but couldn't really focus on them since she was too busy trying to keep the tears at bay. How could he think she was so low? Well, to give him credit, he didn't really know her. All they had between them was sex. Great sex, she corrected. Well, actually, mind blowing sex. Even someone with her limited experience knew that. But that didn't mean she liked the way he treated her.

"I'm sorry," he said, sighing deeply.

Alicia blinked, sure she'd heard him incorrectly. He'd been quiet for so long, she'd assumed that they'd simply finish the dance and return to the table. But with his words, the music changed and he pulled her even closer, his breath gently moving the wisps of hair at her temples.

Alicia glared up at him. "Have you always been so autocratic?" she demanded, her teeth gritting at his irritating smile.

"Of course," he said, chuckling low and deep in his throat. "Have you always been so sexy?" he countered.

"No. And don't change the subject."

"The previous subject bored me."

She rolled her eyes and smothered a smile. Goodness, when he turned on the charm he was merciless. But she didn't want to give in to him that easily. He'd been rude and insulting. "And therefore you must have your way in all things, correct?"

"Absolutely," he replied, grinning unrepentantly.

She watched him for a moment. Then turned her face away before saying, "I don't sleep around. And I wasn't trying to entice Richard." There, she'd said it. Whether he believed her or not, she didn't care.

They danced for a long time and Adam held her close, almost as if he were enjoying simply holding her. Alicia wanted to believe that it might be true. It was definitely accurate on her part. She loved feeling the muscles underneath his dark suit and the expert way he held her and led her through the dance. But she knew it probably wasn't real on his part. She imagined him thinking, working through all the problems to the business deal he had been discussing with the other men over dinner. The man probably didn't know how to stop working.

She looked around, moving slightly closer so she could smell his after shave. It was spicy and so like the man she wanted to taste him. Her eyes glanced up at his and she was caught. The burning look in his eyes told her he was thinking exactly the same thing she was.

Alicia expected to be carted out of the restaurant right at that moment, but it didn't happen. In fact, he pulled her closer himself, his arm wrapping around her waist so her body was almost absorbed into his. Alicia didn't fight the feeling any longer. She laid her head down on his shoulder, her nose almost touching his neck and simply enjoyed being held in his strong arms.

Chapter 7

The phone was ringing on the table next to her and Alicia groaned as she buried her head into the pillow. "Go away," she called out. But nothing happened except the phone continued to ring.

She pulled the pillow off her head angrily, willing the phone to stop ringing. It didn't. "Isn't there an answering machine?" she asked, the ringing starting to really bother her.

After the fifteenth ring, she snatched up the receiver. "Hello!" she said, worried that the caller would be someone important. While she looked around for Adam, she pushed her hair out of her face and lifted the sheet higher over her nakedness.

"Alicia?" Adam's voice came through the receiver.

"Adam? What are you doing calling me?" she asked, puffing the pillow behind her back.

"How else am I going to call you? Where is your cell phone, by the way?" he demanded.

"Cell phone?" she repeated, thinking hard. It was difficult since she was so tired. Adam was a demanding lover and she had been up several times last night. Glancing at the clock, she realized it was only nine o'clock in the morning. She usually woke about nine-thirty or ten o'clock, getting several hours of uninterrupted sleep after Adam left for the office each morning.

54

"Yes, those convenient devices that allow others to reach you when you are out shopping or whatever it is you do," he explained, a tinge of impatience in his tone.

Alicia closed her eyes, squeezing them shut before answering. "Adam, I had it shut off."

"Why the hell would you do that?" he asked after a moment of stunned silence.

She opened her eyes and looked at the ceiling. "I had to shut it off because I don't have any money," she finally admitted. "I let my apartment go as well and sold all of my furniture. Are you happy now? I'm completely penniless and dependent on you. What's next Adam? What's your next phase in my humiliation?"

He actually had the audacity to chuckle. "I told you last week that you only had to ask."

"I'm not in the habit of begging for money," she snapped back.

She heard the deep sigh. "Alicia, I'll set you up with an allowance. But for now, meet me at this restaurant for lunch."

She wrote down the address with the pen and paper he always kept beside the bed. "Fine. Why am I doing this?"

"Because I told you to," he said.

Alicia shook her head. "Believe it or not, I don't actually jump when you say jump," she quipped.

"You do when I touch you in bed," he said, his voice deep and husky. "In fact, I think there was quite a bit of jumping last night when I touched you..."

"Adam stop it," she hissed, furious that her voice was breathy and her heartbeat had already accelerated.

"Stop what?" he chuckled.

"Stop what you were about to say. There's no need to go into any details of what happened last night. It is over and done with," she said, straining to sound businesslike.

"Ah, but that's the thing, my dear. I'm definitely going to do it again so it isn't really done with, now is it?" he said, his voice filled with amusement.

"What's lunch about?" she asked, changing the subject.

"You'll see. Just be here at noon." He was laughing when he hung up the phone and she wished she could slam it into the receiver. The man simply loved embarrassing her, didn't he?

She pulled herself out of bed and got into the shower. Alicia wanted to be late meeting him but she arrived at the restaurant with five minutes to spare. She looked around, intimidated by the immaculate white linen table clothes and beautiful white and pale pink roses as the centerpiece for each table.

Thankfully, Adam walked in right behind her so she didn't have to worry about how to approach the Maitre'd in her serviceable but boring navy suit which was the only thing she had to wear besides the jeans she'd been wearing for the past four or five years.

They were seated immediately and the wine steward arrived with a bottle of white wine, displaying the label to Adam who immediately nodded his head.

"I'll have the usual Jim," Adam said when the waiter walked up.

"Very good, sir," he said. "And for the lady?" he asked, turning to Alicia, eyebrows raised as he waited for her order.

"The lady will have the salmon," Adam said.

"She will?" Alicia asked, stepping into the conversation that had been starting around her. "Why will she have the salmon? She doesn't like salmon," Alicia asked, smiling hugely, feeling wonderful for some reason and more than ready to tease Adam who was trying to order for her.

Adam looked across the table at her. Mockingly he bent his head and waved to the menu that had been placed at her elbow. "By all means, please tell us what you would prefer?" he said.

Alicia quickly glanced through the menu at the lunch items. She felt uncomfortable, knowing that both the waiter and Adam were waiting. She quickly selected the first thing that sounded good. "I'll have the strawberry salad," she said, her mouth watering at the idea of the strawberries and blue cheese on a bed of greens described in the menu.

The waiter bowed solicitously and moved away, allowing the two of them to glare at each other across the table. Alicia was in too good of a mood to continue with the anger contest and she was the first to smile. "Did you have a good morning?" she asked.

"No. How about you?"

Alicia shook her head. "No. This odious man called me up and interrupted my morning sleep in. Then he tried to embarrass me."

Adam leaned his forearms onto the edge of the table and lifted his glass to his lips. "Did it work?" he finally said.

Alicia laughed softly. "Nope. I figured he was just trying to wake me up faster, jealous that I was still in that big, comfortable bed while he was slaving away at some awful company. The owner is really mean," she whispered conspiratorially.

Adam threw back his head and laughed. "Is he?" he finally asked. "Well, you should talk to him about how to manage a company. He can't have very good employee retention, which is always bad for business."

Alicia reluctantly smiled, enjoying his laughter as much as his teasing. They spent the rest of the meal talking about nothing in particular but Alicia loved getting to know him a little more. He was more relaxed, quicker to laugh and less quick to tell her what to do for some reason.

Unfortunately, the lunch ended and Alicia stood up, prepared to leave and head back to his penthouse. "Don't go anywhere," he said as he signed the tab. "We have more stops."

He stood up and put a hand to the small of her back as he led her out of the restaurant. They got into the limousine and Bill apparently already had his instructions. Alicia was overwhelmed when he led her to one of the exclusive New York boutiques. The dresses in the window were worth more than her gross monthly salary, she thought, her eyes huge as she was escorted inside.

A pretty, blond woman with a perfectly tailored suit walked up to greet them. "Good afternoon, Mr. Meyers. We've been expecting you. We have several selections ready for your approval."

"Good. This is Alicia. She'll be making the selections," Adam said.

"Very good, sir. This way," the lady smiled, showing Alicia to the back of the store to where a rack of dresses, slacks, skirts, shirts and evening gowns were hanging. "Mr. Meyers mentioned that he thought you were about a size six or eight," the woman replied, looking Alicia up and down, "But I think you are closer to a size six. Am I right?"

Alicia could only nod her head, her eyes looking at the beautiful gowns.

"Wonderful. Why don't you follow me to the dressing room and we can start with the first outfit?" she suggested, one arm outstretched to indicate a doorway that obviously led to a dressing room.

Alicia stared, worried about the whole expense. She turned to find Adam sitting on a satin covered chair, looking amused.

"Adam, could I have a word with you?" she whispered.

Adam glanced quickly at the sales attendant who immediately moved away, giving them privacy.

"What's wrong?" he asked.

Alicia ignored the amused smile flitting over his features. "Adam, you don't need to do this," she said. "These dresses are too expensive."

"By whose standards?" he asked, the smile lighting his eyes.

"By everyone's!" she gasped.

"Not mine. Besides, it's my money and I'd like to see you in those dresses." His eyes moved over her features and his smile changed from amusement to sensuality. "And out of them," he finished in a huskier voice.

Alicia couldn't help the blush that stole over her features with his comment but she tried to inject a serious note into the conversation. "Adam, this is insane. You can't spend this much money on me. Maybe just a nice sweater or something, but not from here."

Adam couldn't contain his laughter any longer. He took her lips gently, then pulled back, shaking his head. "Alicia, my dear, you are a strange mixture. Go try on the outfits and let me decide what I want to spend my money on."

Her chin jutted out and she crossed her arms over her chest. "No. I can't let you do this. It isn't right."

Adam laughed again. "Alicia, if you don't try them on, I'm going to simply purchase the lot of them and have them delivered for you. And if you don't wear them, I'll take a knife to the other outfits so you have nothing to wear." His eyes lit up, "Just for the record, I'm not opposed to coming home to you completely naked."

Alicia ground her teeth in frustration. "You're impossible," she said and stood up, her hands balled at her hips and glared at him. "I'm doing this out of protest," she said and stomped off to the dressing area.

Three hours later, the trunk to the limousine was completely filled with boxes and bags as well as the passenger seat and all the available space in the back.

"I'm not wearing those undergarments, Adam," she said, her arms crossed over her stomach and her face flaming to a beet red.

Adam laughed at her expression. "Alicia, you're priceless," he said and pulled her onto his lap. His mouth captured hers before he finally pulled away and shook his head. "I've never seen a woman so averse to getting new clothes," he said, his eyes showing his confusion. "I thought all women loved getting new clothes. I didn't mean for this afternoon to be a torturous one for you."

Alicia had her arms wrapped around his neck but she frowned. "It isn't that I don't like the clothes. It's just that they were so expensive."

"So you've mentioned," he said, his voice muffled because his mouth was nibbling on her earlobe.

"Adam, I'm serious," she said, but then gasped when his hand slid up inside her navy coat.

"I'm serious too. I don't want you in this suit anymore. And I'll open up an account at those stores so you can go out and purchase anything you'd like. I have more events planned and you'll need an appropriate dress, a different dress, for each occasion."

She pulled back, her face showing her shock. "You just bought me five new evening gowns. How many more will I need?" she asked, her voice weak with the idea of spending even more of his money.

"I don't know. I'll have to look at my calendar. But tonight, we're dining in," he told her.

Alicia didn't mind that at all. In fact, she was thrilled when he carried her into the bedroom and she wasn't thinking about all the new clothes or their expense for the rest of the night.

The next two weeks were out of a story book, she thought. Adam took her to the opera, the ballet, to dinners with friends and business acquaintances. They danced and Adam showed her a world that she'd never even imagined. It was a world where people glittered and laughed and played hard after a hard day at the office.

What's more, he talked to her more often. He called her from the office on her new cell phone that he'd had delivered, asking her to meet him for lunch. Those times, he talked to her and they argued about everything, with Alicia usually laughing at his blatant charm and arrogant assertion that he was right, even when he knew she'd made an excellent point.

One night, she was laying in his arms while watching a movie. They were spread out over the comfortable sofa, her head resting on his arm for a pillow. The movie ended but both were reluctant to get up.

Alicia felt Adam's hands around her waist, his fingers spread out over her stomach. "Why did your father embezzle the money?" he asked, the ending music from the movie in the background.

Alicia stiffened instantly and her mind whirled. What was he thinking? Was he actually thinking about her? Then she stopped herself. Adam was nothing if not direct. If he wanted to know about her, he'd simply ask. She had to start trusting him at some point. Why not now?

She relaxed in his arms once again and shrugged her shoulders. "I only have my theories. My mother wouldn't let us talk to him in prison, and then he was killed by a fellow inmate. So I was never able to ask him myself."

"What are your theories?" he asked, his fingers lightly brushing her bare skin under her shirt.

Alicia took a deep breath and considered all that she'd known growing up as a teenager. "Like I said, I don't know if this is true or not, but my father always overspent on the household budget. I remember fights with my parents yelling and screaming at each other after Maggie and I had gone to bed. My mother was always furious with my father for spending our money on something silly or superficial. Things he obviously didn't need."

"Such as?" he prompted.

Alicia thought back. "A motorcycle." She grimaced at the memory. "The neighbor across the street got a motorcycle one weekend and was driving around the streets, not even really showing off, just excited about his new toy. My father grumbled all that week, then Saturday morning he disappeared, only to come home that afternoon with a bigger and faster motorcycle. And not only that, he had a new leather jacket, a helmet, leather gloves, all of it. He'd even bought helmets for me and Maggie so we could ride on the back as well."

"What about a helmet for your mother?"

Alicia shook her head. "No. He must have known that she wouldn't touch it."

61

"So what else?"

"Hmmm...I remember one time my mother was going to throw a cookout for some friends. The week before the party, he'd come home each night with something else he absolutely needed for the party. One night it was an ice cream maker, the next, a new grill, new chairs for everyone to sit on. The list just went on and on."

"What did your mother say?"

"At that point in our lives, things weren't so tight so she only smiled and shook her head. I was in about the third or fourth grade, I think. It took a few more years before things really got tight."

"And then what happened?"

Alicia sat up but wouldn't look at him. "Then things weren't tight anymore. The bills were paid, my mother had money to buy us clothes as well as some for herself. She never worried about going to the grocery store. Things were nice for a while."

"But then he got caught."

Alicia reached for the remote to the television to turn it off. "Right. Then he got caught and the police came and took so many things out of the house. They tracked many of the items back to the stolen funds. In the end, we were piled with lawyer's fees and had nothing except beds, a sofa and plates. They even took the kitchen table."

"That must have been hard."

Alicia looked away. She'd never spoken about that time in her life or the humiliation that had come with the process of having her father carted away in handcuffs, then the trial afterwards. "At the time it was happening, I couldn't imagine anything worse than the police coming into our house and destroying everything that made me feel secure. But then I had to go to school the next day. That was even worse. We'd lived in a small town so everyone knew about the charges and that my father was still in jail. They wouldn't let him out on bail, knowing they hadn't recovered all the money."

Adam was silent, waiting, obviously knowing that she wanted to talk about it. "But even that day wasn't the worst."

"What was the worst?" he asked gently.

Alicia was quiet for so long, he wondered if she was going to answer him. She stared out into the dark night, probably not seeing anything but the memories. "The second worst day was when my father was convicted. But even while that moment was bad, I knew it was going to happen. My mother made us come to the trial every day, to show our support for our father. Maggie and I sat there, heard the accusations, heard all the evidence that pointed so obviously to what he'd done."

"And the worst moment?" he asked.

She hesitated, but sighed before saying, "It was right after the trial. My father had just been led out of the courtroom in handcuffs. We came back to the almost empty house, stunned and still in shock, and my mother broke down." She shuddered at the memory. "Seeing her crumble onto the floor, desolate, incapable of helping Maggie or me. It was terrifying."

"So you took care of your sister all those years as well as your mother." It was a statement and the words were filled with understanding.

Alicia turned to face him, her jaw set and her lips tight. "Yes. I took care of all three of us. But I didn't steal any money to do it." She took a deep breath, blinking back the tears that were hovering on her eyelashes. "I would never put anyone through that kind of hell." She glared at him. "So whoever embezzled that money, they are still doing it."

Without another word, she walked into the bedroom. She showered and brushed her teeth, then pulled on an old tee-shirt. Curling into bed, she closed her eyes, willing the painful memories to ease. She hated thinking back to those days. It did no good. The trial had been horrible, seeing her father sitting in the hard, wooden chair, hearing the accusations being flung in his direction. He just sat there, slumped over and looking...pathetic.

Just as much as her father's actions had created the situation, her anger and humiliation during those long, awful months had created this one. She was in this penthouse initially because she would never put her sister through that kind of experience. But also because she was in love with Adam.

The tears eventually fell but she remained silent, even after she felt the bed dip, knowing that Adam had come to bed.

He didn't pull her towards him, obviously respecting the fact that she needed space tonight. It was the first night in more than a month in which he hadn't touched her, made love with her. But Alicia was grateful. If he'd touched her, she might have exploded and she wasn't sure she could pull herself back together.

Adam laid in the bed, knowing that Alicia was crying. Her words sifted through his mind and he tried to come to terms with why she had stolen so much money from him. She'd learned from her father, obviously. It was the same pattern as his thefts but she hadn't flaunted her stolen money with the neighbors. Although there was no trace of her spending the money, he knew it had gone to her sister's education or her mother's care. He sighed heavily, unsure of where to go now. He understood her better but he couldn't reconcile the woman who smiled so easily, but hid so much behind that smile.

Chapter 8

On Saturday of the next week, Adam rolled over and pulled her against his side. "I think it is time we get you out of your jeans and shorts and into something a little more festive."

"What did you have in mind?" she asked, putting her hands on his shoulders, relaxing under his tender gaze.

"I think you should pull on a bathing suit and let's spend the day near the ocean," he said.

"Ocean?" Alicia repeated skeptically.

"Exactly," he replied and climbed out of bed. "You'd better hurry. You'll need to pack."

Alicia sat up on her elbows, completely flabbergasted and confused. "Pack? What happened to spending a day near the ocean?"

His smile was roguish as he gently bit then kissed her shoulder. "Well, we have to get there, don't we?" he said. Without another word, he winked at her, then disappeared into the shower.

Alicia stared after him, wondering what he could possibly be planning. She pulled the sheet back and slid her arms into her silk robe that had been lying on the chair next to the bed. She picked up the shredded, matching silk negligee, shaking her head at how long it had stayed on her body. It was one of those silk pieces that Adam had bought for her that one day he'd taken her shopping.

If her nightgown lasted more than five minutes after she put it on and he saw her in it, that would be a record. She often wondered why she even bothered putting it on but then blushed at the idea of coming to bed naked. That would just be too risqué. She wasn't sure if she was up to that kind of blatant invitation. Not that Adam needed one.

The next seventy-two hours were magical for Alicia. Adam took her to the airport and they boarded his private plane. As soon as they were airborne, Alicia looked over at him and demanded, "Adam, where are we going?"

Adam laughed, knowing that she had been dying of curiosity all morning. "I told you, to the ocean."

Alicia eyed him carefully, considering what her next question would be. "What country is this ocean next to?" she finally asked.

He grinned. "You're learning," he said. "How about Greece?"

Alicia had to laugh at his charming grin. "And what if I said I didn't like Greece?"

"Then we'd turn around and head to the Caribbean."

She smiled at his grin. "I'm sure you've been to hotels all over the world. What's your favorite place to visit?"

"Well I don't actually stay in hotels in either Greece or the Caribbean. But I have to say I like Aruba a great deal. Very nice island. Great food too."

She was stuck on his previous comment. "What do you mean you don't stay in hotels? Where do you stay?"

"I have houses in both countries," he said, matter-of-factly.

Her jaw dropped open in shock. "You have three houses? Do you rent them out when you aren't using them?"

Adam laughed. "No. I don't rent them out although I have friends who use them occasionally. And just so you know, I actually

66

have six houses."

Alicia was gripping the arms of her leather chair. "Six?" she asked, sitting up a little straighter in her chair. "Good grief Adam!" she gasped. "What on earth do you do with six houses?"

"I work hard and I play hard. I like having the conveniences of home whenever possible."

Alicia shook her head. "Adam, I hate to tell you this but you could just pack an extra bag so you'd have all the conveniences of home. You don't actually have to have your own home."

Adam threw back his head and laughed, then pulled her forward. "Alicia, you're very cute when you're being frugal."

She couldn't respond since his mouth covered hers, and with that, all thought of admonishing him for his excessive number of houses flew out the window.

They spent the next three days laying on his private beach in Greece, swimming in the azure water, eating fresh seafood either prepared by a local woman who came in to take care of the house and cook while he was in residence, or going out to the local restaurants. It was a fantasy weekend where nothing mattered except for when to wake up and fall asleep. Adam was an amazing lover, anticipating all of her needs to the point of making sure she had fresh coffee as soon as she woke up, even if he was already out in the ocean swimming for exercise.

He showed her how to snorkel and even gave her diving lessons although they didn't go very deep since she wasn't certified. They explored reefs and caves, laid in the sand letting the sun heat their bodies, wind surfed and just enjoyed being outside and in the fresh air.

It was a complete novelty for Alicia who had spent the last ten years working every day of her life, usually more than one job and sometimes even two extra jobs just to pay all the bills. Spending time simply enjoying herself, being spoiled by the surf and Adam's charm, she felt like a completely different person.

The only cloud hanging over her happiness was the fact that Adam still thought of her as a criminal. She stopped professing her innocence and just accepted that this period in her life was special and she'd simply have to enjoy it until it ended. At that point, she'd figure out how to pick up the pieces of her life and move forward.

Flying back to New York Monday night was almost depressing. The air in Greece had been dry and hot. New York was humid with the chance of rain coming down from the north so it would turn colder with that imminent rain.

It also meant that she wouldn't see Adam every day. In Greece, she could look out her window and find him either in the ocean or on the beach or maybe even sitting on the patio reading the Greek newspaper while sipping the thick, dark coffee. By morning, he'd be back in the office and she'd be all alone, wondering how to fill in her days until Adam came back in the evening.

She hated the fact that she'd fallen in love with the man. For as sure as the sun would come up the next day, Adam would grow tired of her. She was amazed that he hadn't so far. But he would. He wasn't the kind of man who would stay with one woman for long.

But why would she want him to? There was no future with him. She had to keep reminding herself that she was here as part of her "punishment". It was hard to separate herself and her position from her feelings for him.

If only he'd remained the hard, callous man she'd encountered in the office that day, she told herself. That was a man she desired, but definitely didn't like. Getting to know him had also changed her feelings and that would only create heartache down the road.

Gone was the hard and demanding lover of the first week. Adam she found, was a very sweet man, free with compliments and full of humor. After coming home, his first priority was always making love. Sometimes it was fast and furious and other times it was so slow and painfully sweet she was almost in tears and begging him to give her body the release it needed. After making love, they usually heated up whatever Gerald had left for them and he would tell her about his day, relaying the silly or impractical ideas that had come across his desk, ready with very dry sarcasm as he talked to her about the foibles of the business world.

She listened intently, loving the way he shared his day with her but also wishing she had something to share with him as well. She'd always loved numbers and the story they told but she also remembered her high school love of writing.

That memory stirred within her that first morning back from Greece. She looked out the window at the bright, morning sunshine as she sipped her strong coffee and considered her options. She could mope around the house feeling sorry for herself and being lonely because she didn't have anyone to talk to. Or she could occupy her time doing something that she'd probably never have a chance to do again in her life. Adam was taking care of all of her living expenses. Why couldn't she start writing something?

She actually had no idea what she'd write but the thought of putting her mind to use, generating something creative and challenging, enticed her. Her mind worked through all the possible issues, then figured out how to get around them. There weren't many problems except the need for a computer and a plot.

The plot she could easily take care of. She searched Adam's office, initially feeling guilty for going through his desk. But she found a pad of lined paper and a pen, then took her coffee out to the terrace and started jotting down notes.

It was time for lunch before she stopped and realized she'd filled up almost ten pages of notes. Towards the end, she'd even started writing out the dialog and building the characters. She made herself a sandwich and carried her notebook to the park, continuing to write down more thoughts, more ideas and building up the images of her scenes and characters.

The next morning, right after Adam left for the office, Alicia quickly showered and changed into her jeans and a tee-shirt. Adam was extremely generous with his money and had given her a lump sum for spending on whatever she pleased. But she hadn't spent any of it yet, not knowing anything she wanted to buy that he had not already gotten for her. So she was going to buy a computer!

She didn't need anything too strong but wanted something reliable. At the computer store, she spoke with the salesperson and finally was talked into buying a lower-priced laptop since she didn't need the gaming technology that was important to others. She was so excited, she hurried home and set it up, proud of herself for being able to do the task on her own. Generally, she was pretty inept when it came to computer problems.

But as her fingers smoothed over the top of the keyboard, ready to start writing, she had no idea what she wanted to write.

"Yoo-hoo!" a male voice said from the doorway.

"Hi!" Alicia said, flustered as Gerald walked into the penthouse, loaded down with groceries. "I wasn't expecting you for another hour," she said and rushed over to help him carry everything into the kitchen.

"Well, I thought about what we were talking about last week and brought you some extra ingredients," he announced, then laughed at her shocked expression. "Oh, don't assume that everyone is as insensitive as that awful man you're living with," he said in his usual casual manner.

"Adam is insensitive?" she repeated out loud, following behind him.

"Sure he is. He's the only one I cook for and he only eats about half of whatever I make for him. At least until you showed up and now everything has been gone by the end of the week." He looked back and winked at her. "I guess you're keeping him in instead of going out to all those fancy restaurants the other women used to drag him to," he chuckled.

Alicia blushed because he was right. She and Adam had been spending most nights in. In bed, that is. After making love, they would shower and heat up whatever was left in the refrigerator for that night.

Gerald tsked approvingly at her reaction. "Lovely blush, my dear girl which is extremely telling," he said and started unloading the groceries. "But suffice it to say, I have been cooking for your hunky man for over five years and he has never said thank you or even told me what his preferences were in foods. I'm constantly guessing. And since he never tells me that one meal or another was good, I have no clue. About two years ago, I gave up trying to entice the man and now just throw together whatever I feel like cooking," he explained, busily laying out the ingredients for the next week's meals.

Alicia was astonished that Gerald really was hurt by Adam's lack of communication. She thought back to the recent meals they had shared. "I know he liked the chicken you cooked last week," she said.

Gerald stilled and looked back at her. "The chicken with the white wine sauce?" he asked hopefully.

Alicia nodded. "But I don't think he likes fruit in his salads," she mentioned, remembering how Adam had pushed the mandarin oranges off to the side one night. She'd thought the spinach with oranges and a sweet and sour dressing had been delicious but she didn't pay for the food or preparation.

Gerald looked crushed for a moment. But it only took a moment for his sunny disposition to spark back to life. "Well, at least it is something," he replied, instantly moving again to finish unloading the food onto the counter.

"Well, this week, I'm making some luscious dinners that will be very romantic," he explained. "And you, my dear, are going to learn the fine art of making chocolate chip cookies."

Alicia instantly perked up. "Really?" she asked, more interested in the cookies than the romantic meals he was considering.

"Of course." He reached into his last bag and pulled out a piece of paper. "While I cook the meals, you stay over there and whip us up some cookies. I'll let you know if you are doing anything wrong or answer any questions."

She stared at the ingredients warily. "I thought the first thing to try was pie since it was so simple."

Gerald shook his head. "Darling, whoever thought up the phrase 'easy as pie' was simply sadistic. Pies are almost impossible to make correctly. The crust has to be flaky but not too dry, the insides have to have just enough oomph for them to stick together but not be mushy," he explained. Waving his hand in the air dramatically, he laughed and said, "Leave the pie making to the more dedicated chefs and trust me." He pointed to the mixing bowl. "Make the cookies."

Alicia read through the instructions determinedly. "If you're sure," she said.

They worked on opposite sides of the counter for the rest of the afternoon. After about an hour and two cookie sheets destroyed, Gerald was whipping up a brandy sauce. "Here, love. You've got to relax a little," he said, handing her a glass of brandy.

"I'm not sure alcohol is the best answer to successful cookie baking," she said but took a tentative sip anyway. Gerald was the expert so who was she to question his instructions. By the time the fourth sheet of cookies came out of the oven, she wasn't even bothered by the fact that the bottoms were black. She was making progress since the tops weren't black.

"What am I doing wrong, Gerald? The time on the instructions say that they should only be in for ten minutes but they are all burning," she said, taking another long sip of brandy and almost missing the counter as she plunked the sheet down in frustration.

"You're probably putting them too close to the bottom of the oven. Don't get discouraged, dear. Just keep trying."

Gerald was already finished with the meals and had completely cleaned up the kitchen when her first batch of cookies came out perfectly. "Look!" she yelled, jumping up and down in her excitement. "I can't believe it. They are perfect!"

"Good girl! Now finish off that batch of cookies before the sun sets," he teased.

Alicia put down the cookie sheet and lifted off the first few cookies, carefully placing them on the cooling rack just as Gerald had shown her earlier in the afternoon. "Well, this has been amazing. What can you teach me next week?" she asked, biting her lip as she delicately offloaded the cookies, careful to not let them break.

"What the hell is going on in here?" a deep voice demanded from the kitchen doorway.

Alicia screamed and her hand automatically flew up in to the air. Gerald, understanding what she had been in the process of doing since

72

he was leaning over her shoulder watching her, ducked immediately. He easily avoided the flying cookie. Adam, who was looking like the wrath of the devil, didn't even flinch as the cookie landed on the wall only inches from his ear.

"Adam!" Alicia called out, horrified that she'd almost smacked him with a cookie but excited to share her achievement with him. "Come look! I've finally succeeded!"

He didn't look too enthused by her excitement. In fact, he looked even angrier. "Yes, Adam. Who were you expecting? Or should I say, not expecting?"

Alicia shook her head. "What are you talking about?" she asked, then waved him closer. "Come over and see what I've made!"

Gerald, who understood exactly what was going on inside his client's mind, quickly picked up his gear and moved towards the door. "Alicia dear, I'll see you next week. You've done a wonderful job and we'll work on maybe a casserole next week," he said. "If I'm still employed, that is," he muttered and squeezed out of the kitchen.

Alicia gazed unsteadily after him, not sure she understood what was going on. "Why would he wonder something like that?" she asked Adam who had started to walk forward.

"Because he might be fired," he said, a muscle twitching on the side of his face.

Her smile as well as her balance was a little wobbly due to the brandy she'd imbibed during her cookie making lesson. "Why would he be fired? He's a wonderful cook and you love most of his meals."

"What the hell were you doing here with him this afternoon?" he demanded, both hands on his hips.

Alicia stared at him, her mind slowly clearing of the brandy induced haze as she realized he was genuinely angry. "Adam, what exactly are you implying?" she asked, putting the cookies down onto the cooling rack and taking off her oven mitts.

"Perhaps I'm not being clear enough. What was that man doing in here with you alone?"

Alicia finally understood, then slapped a hand over her mouth, trying to stifle her laughter. "Adam, please tell me you didn't think that me and Gerald..." she couldn't finish the sentence but started laughing instead. "Oh, Adam. That's ridiculous."

Adam didn't like being laughed at. He grabbed her shoulders and pulled her against him. "While you're paying off this debt, you're mine. Do you understand me?" he said harshly. "I don't care what you do once our agreement is over with but you are my exclusive property in the meantime."

Adam took a step away from her and turned away, then just as quickly turned back, picked her up into his arms with her feet flying in the air. She had only moments to grab his shoulders before he was walking determinedly towards the bedroom.

"Adam, what are you planning?" she asked, becoming slightly nervous when he didn't answer. He was angrier than she'd ever seen him. Angrier than she'd ever seen anyone in her life. He controlled it well, but she could feel the anger under her fingertips.

"Take off your clothes," he demanded, setting her on her feet and kicking the door closed. His hand went to his tie and pulled it off, tossing it to the floor. His jacket followed and he didn't even care that the beautifully tailored jacket was in a crumpled heap on the floor of his bedroom.

Alicia backed away, watching him carefully. "Adam, I think we should talk about this," she said, holding up her hands in front of her. But each step she took backwards, he took one towards her. Suddenly, her legs were against the bed and she was trapped. The dark look in his eyes told her what his intentions were and she was tingling with excitement and not a small amount of fear.

"I don't think we should talk at all. I think you should do as I say," he demanded. By that point, the buttons were undone on his shirt as it hung loose around his waist. He reached out and grabbed one of her wrists, then pulled her close to him.

Alicia could barely think when her hands touched his heated skin. She wanted him. There was no denying it. When his mouth came down on hers it was hard and demanding, almost brutal. She cried out softly, and her hand reached up to touch his face. Instantly, the kiss changed from angry to coaxing. He lifted his mouth and stared down into her soft, blue eyes that showed her hurt as well as her excitement. With a groan, he pulled her closer to his body and lifted her into his arms, putting her down onto the bed.

His lovemaking that night was different. It was more intense, almost as if he was trying to show her that he was the only man who could make her feel these kinds of feelings. It was overwhelming and by the time he entered her, she was so desperate for release, she was begging him to take her.

By morning, he was gone and Alicia rolled over onto her stomach, staring out into the morning sunshine. "What am I going to do?" she asked the empty apartment.

Laying her head down on the pillow, she looked at the ceiling and thought about her dreams and what she had been hoping would happen by this point in her life. She remembered laying in her bed as a little girl and thinking about dating in high school, going to the prom, or other high school dances. It was such a long time ago, she thought in amazement. She didn't notice that she was crying until she felt the tear slide down her cheek.

What was it about her life that she was constantly being punished? She wasn't sure if she was strong enough for this, she thought to herself.

The ringing phone brought her out of her moment of self pity. She wiped her face with the back of her hand and reached for the phone. It was odd to hear it ringing since no one called Adam here. Anyone trying to reach him would call his mobile instead of his home phone

"Hello?" she said tentatively, worried about answering his phone. But she didn't even care if it was a salesperson. She needed human contact.

"Alicia? Did I wake you?" Adam asked.

Alicia sat back on the pillows, amazed that his authoritarian personality could reach through the phone. "No. I've been up for a few minutes," she explained.

"Good. Listen, I'm sorry about the short notice but we're going to have to go away this weekend," he said.

"Really?" she asked, the thought instantly exciting her.

"Yes. You'll need new clothes though. I've arranged for you to get a few things over at a store Bill will take you to. He's on his way back to pick you up."

"What kinds of things and where are we going?"

"To my house in the country. I have some friends who are coming into town. Do you think you could handle that? No stealing the family jewels, okay?" he asked.

Alicia made a face, grateful that he couldn't see it. "I'm glad you have such faith in me," she replied sarcastically, her hands picking up the soft, cotton sheet and dropping it again. "If you're worried that I'll be an embarrassment, why in the world would you want to take me?"

"You can ask me that after last night?" he chuckled.

Her face turned red with embarrassment. Even after several weeks, she still didn't understand how he could change her so dramatically with his simple touch. "I guess I am rather convenient," she said stiffly.

"That you are. And lovely to boot. So be a good girl and go get dolled up. I'll pick you up at three so you don't have much time and you have a lot to buy. Have fun," he said and hung up the phone.

Alicia stared at the dead receiver, furious with him for his insensitive words and how unfair it was that she was being accused of something before she'd even gotten out of bed. But she remembered all the evidence in that file folder. If she'd come across that amount of evidence, she'd feel pretty good about the case against the person.

Sighing, she pulled back the sheets and slipped into the tee-shirt that had fallen to the floor in last night's wild passion. She picked up the rest of the clothes that were still scattered all over the carpet, grimacing when her muscles protested. She certainly didn't need to work out when she had Adam in her life, she thought. He definitely kept her exercised.

The shower was wonderful and each time she stepped into it, she felt better, cleaner both inside and out. She wished she could do the same thing with her mind and her heart. She wondered how much longer Adam would continue this farce of a relationship. He'd mentioned a month for every ten thousand dollars he claimed she'd stolen from him but how much had the real criminal actually stolen? She could only hazard that it was a lot.

She dried her hair and piled it loosely up on her head with a clip. She looked at her reflection in the mirror and wondered where Adam had set up an account for her. Her tee-shirt and jeans were extremely well worn. She wondered if they would take one look at her and kick her out of the boutique as if she were a beggar.

Alicia smiled at the idea and shrugged her shoulders, strapping on her watch and one of her two pairs of earrings. They were a simple gold bead dangling from a hoop. They had been inexpensive but had looked nice at the time she'd bought them but now they were a little tarnished. If she were still working and had an income, she would go out and purchase a new pair. Her only other pair were simple, silver hoops. The two pairs alternated each day or with her outfits.

Sighing, she shook her head at her reflection. She certainly didn't look like the kind of person who moved in the same circles as Adam who had immaculately tailored suits and beautiful silk ties. She suspected that one of his shoes cost more than her entire old wardrobe. She could have chosen one of the other outfits Adam had bought her but she didn't feel right wearing them when he wasn't around. She knew she was being silly, but she just couldn't help herself.

"See you later, Joe," Alicia called to the doorman as she walked through the white, marble lobby.

"Going for a walk?" he called back to her, tipping his hat.

"Not this time. I've got a shopping spree planned," she laughed, waving to him as Bill held the door for her.

"You have a good time then," he said.

"Thanks. See you in a while,"

She ducked her head into the back of the limousine, smiling to Bill who closed the door after her.

"Where are we off to, Bill?" she asked, leaning back into the soft, leather seats of the car.

"Mr. Meyers asked me to drive you to Barney's, ma'am."

"Just call me Alicia, Bill," she said, not for the first time. But the man was a stickler for protocol. "Barney's sounds expensive."

"I'm sure you'll find something that you like," he teased. "Are you excited about the weekend?"

"Not really. Adam only mentioned that we were going to his country house. But I don't know where it is."

"It is a beautiful home in Martha's Vineyard, right on the cliffs. You'll love it," he said reassuringly.

A few minutes later, they pulled up outside a large department store. Alicia took a deep breath and stepped out, prepared to be poked and prodded.

She was pleasantly surprised when a friendly woman in her thirties walked up to her upon entry. "Are you Alicia Morgan?" she asked, smiling pleasantly.

"Yes," Alicia replied, rubbing suddenly sweaty palms down the sides of her jeans. The store was beautiful with clothes just as amazing as the last time she'd gone shopping with Adam.

"It's very nice to meet you, Ms. Morgan," the woman said. "I'm Rebecca and Mr. Meyers called and asked me to help you select some outfits."

"I'm not sure..." she started to say, worried that there had been some mistake.

"Don't worry about anything," Rebecca replied reassuringly. "I understand what the weekend entails and I've already selected some outfits for your review. But if none appeal to you, there are many more styles and colors." Rebecca was efficiency personified. "If you'll come this way, I've arranged for a private room for you," she said.

Alicia couldn't think of anything else to say. She followed Rebecca through the store, her hungry, fashion starved gaze caressing the lovely outfits sitting on the racks or mannequins as she walked through the store. She longed to reach out and touch the incredible fabrics but didn't want to be obvious about her naiveté towards this kind of shopping.

"Here we are. I hope you don't mind but I've requested tea for you as well," she explained, her hand waving over a silver tea set. "Why don't you take a seat and I'll bring out some of the outfits so you can choose which you'd like to try on first."

This was a completely different shopping experience than Alicia had ever had in her life. Usually, she had to go through the sales racks and mix and match jackets or blouses to find something that looked tailored and professional for work. Most of the clothes were out of season as well.

"Here we go," Rebecca said and brought out several outfits.

Alicia was in heaven. She sipped strong tea while shirts, tops, evening gowns and day clothes were brought out for her, all in her size. Alicia chose several quickly but Rebecca wouldn't let her stop with only what was needed for the weekend. She explained that several alternative outfits were requested since the weekend was to be free of restrictions.

With Rebecca's help, three hours later, Alicia was the excited owner of several sophisticated, beautiful new outfits including a figure hugging evening gown in soft green that wrapped around her waist, creating a suggestive V, then flowing out to a graceful waterfall of chiffon and another in a sleek, black silk strapless dress that didn't reveal anything but her arms and shoulders but held her figure lovingly. It would be exciting to wear both dresses, as well as the other outfits that were masterpieces of design and fabric engineering.

"Might I also suggest a quick trip to the salon?" Rebecca offered smoothly. "Perhaps a slight trim to get your hair into a sleeker style?"

Alicia eyed her hair which was pinned up on her head right at the moment. "Oh, I don't think Adam would pay for something like that," she said.

"I think if it was the right style, he'd like it," she suggested. "We won't cut it short, just shape it slightly. I'm sure George could add a touch of color as well. Nothing too dramatic but just enough to enhance the natural shine. What do you say?"

Alicia bit her lower lip. What Rebecca was suggesting sounded wonderful but could she? Should she?

Two hours later, Alicia was weighed down with bags that were quickly loaded into the trunk of the long, black car, her hair styled so that it curled softly around her shoulders.

As soon as she walked into the penthouse, she knew that Adam was there. She could feel him when he was near and that feeling alone scared her. What would happen in a few weeks? Would she become addicted to the man? But how could she? The man hated her. He considered her no better than a criminal, or worse, a prostitute since he was having her pay off her, or someone's, debt in bed. But there was no getting around the fact that her body wanted him and her heart was completely tuned to him on so many levels.

A moment later, he walked out of the bedroom and looked up from the newspaper he'd been reading. His eyes widened slightly, then narrowed as he took in her whole appearance. His perusal was stunned as he looked at her hair, her tee-shirt that didn't have threadbare areas and the slim fitting khakis that she'd worn home from the store instead of her usual well-worn jeans that she'd owned for the past five years.

"Do you like it?" she asked, one hand reaching up to touch her newly styled hair. That was the part that made her the most nervous, she knew. He'd only given her permission to buy new clothes. What would he say about the extra expense?

She decided to get it out in the open, free herself from his painful gaze. "I'm sorry about the expense. The lady at the store recommended it but you obviously don't like it and I'm sorry I spent your money on something other than clothes," she said, her shoulders sagging. "I'll go put these away," she said, trying to lift her spirits up.

"No," his one, harsh word stopped her. "I like it." He walked away, tossing the newspaper onto the sofa as he passed to the bar. He poured himself a large glass of bourbon and tossed it back, hissing as the liquid burned down his throat. "You'll need to pack that stuff up. We leave in fifteen minutes."

Alicia nodded quickly and hid her eyes. Otherwise, he'd see the anger flashing in them. She didn't really want to get into an argument with him. He didn't seem like he was in a good mood and she was, or had been, so she just left him standing there, fuming silently as she went into the bedroom and pulled out her old, beaten up suitcase.

Adam watched Alicia walk to the bedroom. He'd noticed the flash of anger and almost smiled. Almost. His humor was washed away as he watched her walk, his body instantly responding to the gentle sway of her hips, the graceful glide. Her shoulders were back and her head held high and he wanted to call out and apologize. But he didn't trust himself.

Dammit! The moment she'd walked into the room, he'd wanted to pin her down to the sofa and make love to her. And then he'd noticed her hair. He had no idea what she'd done to it but it looked sexy as hell! He had enough trouble concentrating and she had to go and do something to pretty herself up even more? Was she just teasing him? Did she know the effect she had on him and wanted to punish him?

No woman should have that kind of power over him, he told himself. He would just have to gain some self-discipline around her. And that had to start right now. He poured himself another glass of bourbon and swallowed it quickly, hoping the pain would snap his mind out of the funk it had been in since he'd walked into the penthouse and she hadn't been there.

He'd been angry, he realized suddenly. Over the past several weeks, he'd become used to the idea of Alicia being here when he came home. Even if it was late at night, he still liked to smell her as he slipped under the sheets, cover his body with hers. Some nights, he had the intention of only holding her while he fell into an exhausted sleep. But as soon as he touched her soft, silken skin, his body would not allow him to leave her in sleep. He had to possess her, put his stamp on her. She was like a drug. And he had no intention of trying to find a cure.

Forget the idea of gaining some discipline around her. What he needed to do was work her out of his system.

"Are you ready to go?" he called out.

She appeared in the doorway, lugging her suitcase behind her.

"Put that down," he snapped, walking quickly over to her and taking the heavy case out of her hands. "Bill will take care of that," he grumped. Just the smell of her hair, all soft and smelling like flowers, made him harden painfully. He wanted to just sink his fingers into her hair and his body into her softness. But he held back. He was looking forward to having her relatively alone for the weekend. He wasn't concerned about her being with his friends at his country house. She would behave or she'd pay for it. And he'd watch her like a hawk. If she even tried to steal one thing, he'd....

Adam didn't know what he'd do but he vowed he'd keep her out of trouble.

"Let's go," he said and walked out the door. Bill appeared a moment later and picked up their suitcases. He followed Adam and Alicia out the door and into the car.

The drive to his country house was done in almost complete silence. For two hours, Alicia stared out of the window in the back of the long, sleek car and watched the countryside pass by while she listened to Adam conduct business on the phone beside her. Despite her anger with him, she was impressed with the extent of his knowledge. He seemed to be able to recall facts and figures off the top of his head and he went through endless calls on various subjects. Most of the subjects she had no idea what he was talking about.

When Bill turned the corner into a long driveway, Alicia gasped in surprise. Adam's country house wasn't what most people would call a house. It was more along the lines of an estate! The gracious looking mansion with the weathered stones was out of some sort of historical romance novel, complete with turrets on both ends and pointed windows on three stories. The structure was massive and elegant, just like Adam himself.

"Ready?" Adam asked when she didn't get out of the car immediately.

Alicia jumped and pulled herself forward. "Yes, I'm sorry," she gasped, opening the door before Bill had a chance to do it himself.

Adam didn't show her around. Instead, he led her up the long, winding stair case, right into the large, master bedroom. Alicia stood there while Bill placed their cases beside the bed.

"I took the liberty of phoning ahead and Lord and Lady Marshall have already arrived," he said, before backing out of the room.

"Lord and Lady Marshall?" Alicia asked, awed and suddenly nervous.

Adam glanced back at her and immediately noticed the anxiety in her eyes. "Yes. They're my friends who are staying here this weekend." He walked over to her and kissed her hard. "I guess that means we should go greet them instead of letting me show you around the house. I'll show you around later, eh? And I'll end with the bed over there."

Alicia's knees were already weak as he touched her lips, his hand skimming over her back and ribs to rest just under her breasts. "I guess so," she gasped.

"What would you rather do?" he asked, dipping his head to nibble on her throat.

Alicia wanted to yell at him for ignoring her so completely for the past two hours, working during the entire drive and being completely inconsiderate. But with his lips brushing against her skin, nibbling on her earlobe, she couldn't argue. She could barely think except to wonder about the amazing things he could make her body feel.

The voice came from a distance but it was booming nonetheless. "Meyers! Break up whatever you've been doing and get down here!"

Alicia jumped slightly but Adam only lifted his head and sighed heavily.

"A friend of yours?" Alicia asked, embarrassed that her voice sounded husky and uneven. She tried to take a step backwards, put a little space between their bodies but he wouldn't let her.

"Not anymore," he growled.

"Meyers! I know you're here. I just saw Bill leave so come on down!" the voice boomed again.

Alicia laughed softly. "I don't think we're going to get any peace until you show yourself."

Adam rested his chin on the top of her head and sighed again. "What was I thinking to invite them for the weekend?" he asked rhetorically.

"I gather they aren't close friends?" she asked tentatively.

Adam shook his head. "Actually, they are two of my best friends. I just don't want them around right at this moment," he replied. Taking a deep breath, he stepped back and took her hand. "But I guess there's no way out of it at this point in the game. We'd better head downstairs or they'll come up looking for us. At least Gary will. Eleanor has more manners than to intrude."

Alicia laughed again, thrilled with the frustration she could see in his eyes. It felt wonderful to know that she had put that frustration there.

During their whole relationship so far, she had felt like a puppet guided by his strings. Each time he touched her, she was his willing partner. And now, he was showing her that she wasn't the only one. Well, at least at this moment in time. He'd be back in control soon, she wagered. Adam wasn't the kind of man that would allow anyone to have control for very long.

She felt a warm glow come over her as he led her down the stairs. This time, he didn't put a proprietary hand at the small of her back. He wasn't demanding something from her either. He was guiding her down the stairs with his fingers laced through hers, as if he really wanted her company.

"It's about time, old man," the deep, booming voice said as they rounded the corner and entered a large, beautifully decorated great room.

The room had a two story stone wall that could be intimidating but because of a decorator's gentle and creative touch, the atmosphere was cozy and intimate. Alicia instantly fell in love with the room as well as the amazing view out of the windows that lined one wall of the great room. The cliffs of Martha's Vineyard were spectacular. The waves were crashing against the sand in the distance and farther out, she could see the wind whipping the water into white frothy tops. She'd heard about the beautiful beaches on the island but had never had the chance to come out and see them before.

"Nice view, huh?" a soft, feminine voice said from beside her.

Alicia tore her eyes away from the windows and looked at the woman next to her. She was stunning!

The woman extended her hand towards Alicia and smiled. "I'm Eleanor. And this obnoxious brute is my husband, Gary. I'm assuming you are Alicia, am I correct?" she asked, her expression filled with genuine friendliness.

"Yes. It's a pleasure to meet you," Alicia said, taking the other woman's proffered hand. "And you're right, the view is amazing."

"I couldn't agree with you more. I keep asking Gary to buy this place off of Adam but you're man is just selfish and won't even discuss a price."

"Can't put a price on relaxation, Eleanor," Adam said, engulfing the woman in a gentle hug.

Alicia stepped back and tried to hide the jealousy that coursed through her mind and body when Adam touched the beautiful woman. But Eleanor caught the look and smiled reassuringly.

"I think the boys are off to play a round of tennis. How about if we grab ourselves a couple of cold drinks and head for the pool, Alicia?" she suggested, moving to stand by her husband and put a hand on his arm.

Alicia got the message. Eleanor was completely infatuated with her husband and was no threat. Taking a deep breath to calm herself, Alicia acknowledged that she had over-reacted. Her only saving grace at the moment was that Adam hadn't seen her reaction.

"That sounds lovely but you'll have to guide me to the pool. I'm afraid I've never been here before."

Eleanor's eyes showed her surprise. "Really?" She looked over at Adam. "Shame on you for keeping this place a secret. This is a gem. But go get on your bathing suit and I'll meet you back down here in a few minutes. These boys have to discuss terms so they'll take a little while longer."

Alicia looked over at Adam who imperceptibly nodded his head. When she smiled slightly, he winked at her, telling her without words not to worry about the afternoon.

Alicia turned away and started up the stairs after Eleanor. Why had he done that? Adam was turning out to be a completely different man here in the country than he was in New York. She would have to guard herself against him. This lover-like attention could really go to her head.

Pulling on one of her new bathing suits, Alicia surveyed her figure in the mirror. She had always been slim since food had never been in abundance after her father's conviction. But now she could see that she'd lost a great deal of weight over the past few weeks. She imagined the stress of the past month, being considered an embezzler, would do that to a person.

Shaking her head in disgust, she grabbed a fluffy white towel out of the bathroom and headed back downstairs. She opened the door to the bedroom just as Adam was walking in.

His eyes flashed angrily as he looked up and down her body. "Where the hell are you going dressed like that?" he demanded.

Alicia looked down at her bathing suit. It was relatively conservative she thought. The simple black maillot covered her in all the appropriate places although she knew that it hugged her curves. But all bathing suits do that.

"What's wrong with my bathing suit?" she asked, putting her hands on her hips. So long to the lover, back was the arrogant, domineering man who wanted to control each aspect of her life. "You should be happy about the suit," she said, raising her chin slightly.

"Why is that?" he asked, slamming the door behind him impatiently. His eyes darkened and he took a step towards her. Then another.

Alicia stood her ground. She was not going to be intimidated by him this time. There was nothing wrong with her suit and he knew it. He was just being annoying. "Because there's no place to hide anything I steal. Shouldn't you have guessed that by now? I did it just for you!"

Adam snaked one arm around her waist and brought her scantily clad body closer to his. "Is that so? Is that the only reason you bought something so skimpy?" he asked, his tone showing her his anger.

Alicia tried to wriggle out of his tight hold but there was no way to get out of it. So she put her arms around his neck to make herself more comfortable. "First of all, it isn't skimpy. It is perfectly acceptable compared to some of the other bathing suits I could be wearing. And secondly, I didn't buy it. You did. So if you don't like it, tough."

"Is that so?" he repeated, his tone had softened and this really did intimidate her. "Well then, I guess it is my prerogative to demand that you take it off and put on something less revealing."

"You could demand but since I don't have anything less revealing, the alternative might be a little more risqué," she said, her chin going up a notch in challenge. "What's it to be, Adam? This bathing suit or...?"

Adam's eyes narrowed at her defiant expression. "You're in a pretty awkward situation, aren't you?" he asked.

"Not at all," she replied, lifting her shoulder gently. "We all have options. As I see it, I can go downstairs and talk with your friend, Eleanor in this perfectly reasonable bathing suit and play nice," she said smoothly. "Or I can stay inside where their wallets and your silver are stored. While you and your friend Gary are out playing tennis, I could rob the three of you blind and no one would be the wiser until we got back to New York." She tilted her head slightly, as if contemplating something. "I think I have plenty of space in my suitcase," she said, her blue eyes flashing mischievously up at his dark, angry look.

Adam wasn't sure what he wanted to do first to this lovely minx who threw him for a loop at almost every turn. He wanted to teach her a lesson for teasing him but he heard Gary's door closing and knew they wouldn't have much time before his friend was banging on the door.

"You're awfully saucy today, aren't you?" he asked, releasing her a moment later. He pulled off his shirt and walked towards the wardrobe that was already filled with clothes he kept here at the house because he certainly didn't bring a large enough suitcase to have held an entire closet full of outfits. "But don't think this conversation is over. We'll discuss it later tonight," he called out.

Alicia almost laughed but then she saw his bare back and her mouth went dry. Just at that moment, someone knocked on the door and she picked up her towel and walked to the door quickly. "I'm not worried," she said, not looking at him any longer. Otherwise, she wouldn't get out of the room, much less get to the pool.

Eleanor was waiting at the bottom of the stairs, a huge floppy hat on her head, chic sunglasses and a bright, yellow bathing suit with a smart looking sarong tied neatly at her waist. Alicia wished she'd had a perfect ensemble but she had to be satisfied with the extremely comfortable bathing suit she'd bought earlier in the day.

"Ready?" Eleanor called up to her, stuffing several more magazines into a matching yellow bag. "I've asked Rosa to bring us some drinks."

"Who is Rosa?" Alicia asked as she descended the stairs.

"That's Adam's housekeeper and she is also the most amazing cook you'll ever find. She's priceless."

"Does she stay here all the time?"

"She lives in the village and only comes to the house when Adam is out but she also maintains the house. Her husband maintains the yard and is in love with Adam since Jerry is allowed to do anything he wants with the grounds."

They walked down a stone pathway that was surrounded on both sides with flowering bushes and weeping willow trees. Suddenly, the path opened up to a lovely pool bordered on all sides by flowers, potted flowering bushes and trees that seemed to bend over the patio, creating almost a canopy at one end of the pool. There was a waterfall at the other end and a bubbling hot tub on the opposite side. Chairs surrounded the pool in strategic areas and Alicia could see the tennis court about fifty feet away.

"This is lovely," Alicia said, spreading her towel out onto a dark green chaise lounge.

"I agree. Adam loves it here. I don't know why he lives in New York when he could spend more time out here. But I guess it's because he likes the cut throat world of business. Gary used to be like that."

"What changed him?" Alicia asked, more curious than she wanted to admit.

Eleanor smiled nostalgically. "I did. I showed him that there was more to life than work. Now he works hard, but he comes home at a reasonable hour and we travel a lot. He's a much more likeable fellow these days."

Alicia absorbed the other woman's words and wondered what could possibly slow Adam down. He seemed driven in all aspects of his life. Even his lovemaking, if she could call it that since he wasn't in love with her, was like a powerful force that overwhelmed every part of her body.

Eleanor was a wonderful companion. She questioned Alicia on her relationship with Adam but when Alicia couldn't really answer her, she moved on, talking about the history of the house and of the village, filling Alicia in on the silly gossip.

Meanwhile, Alicia watched as Adam and Gary walked through the pool area, tennis racquets in hand as they moved off towards the tennis courts. Alicia was mesmerized when they started playing. Both men were equally skilled at the game and both played to win. It was as if they put their whole life into winning just that serve, that game.

Alicia enjoyed watching the play of muscles across Adam's back and arms, his legs flexing as he reached for a low ball or sprinting across the court to return a more difficult shot. It was like a dance in a way, she thought as Adam and Gary volleyed back and forth.

"So when did you fall in love with him?" Eleanor asked.

Alicia started and looked away, only to have her eyes drawn right back to Adam's incredible form as he served the ball. "Excuse me?" she asked, sure she hadn't heard Eleanor correctly.

"It's all over your face," Eleanor said, laughing softly. "You're in love with him. How long have you been in this crazy state?"

Alicia's mouth dropped open. "I'm not in love with Adam."

Eleanor laughed softly. "Then why can't you tear your eyes away from him?" she asked, one eyebrow raised in a gentle query. "And why are you holding your breath each time he almost misses the ball?"

"Oh!" Alicia said, shaking her head in denial. "That's only fascination. I'm not... Adam's not..." she faltered. Alicia didn't know how to explain the situation. "We're just convenient," she finished lamely.

Eleanor watched for another moment, noting how Alicia's eyes darted right back to Adam. She smiled and slid her sunglasses higher on her nose and allowed her eyes to drift back to her own husband. "He's only tough on the outside, you know," she said.

That got Alicia's attention. "What do you mean?"

Eleanor's smile faded slightly. "He's been hurt by women in the past," he said. "Not because he's been in love but simply because he hasn't found anyone worthy of love. He thinks women are silly and pointless; not for anything serious. Too many women have tried to corner him into marriage, tricking him in one way or another."

Alicia's hands clenched into a fist and her teeth clenched. "Why would they do that?"

Eleanor hid her smile at Alicia's instantaneous anger on Adam's behalf. "Because he's impossibly wealthy, painfully handsome and incredibly powerful. That's a strong aphrodisiac for many women. But he's also razor sharp and not willing to let a woman make a fool of him. He'll try and maintain control. But what he really needs, even if he won't accept it, is a woman who loves him for himself and not for all the things she can get from him."

Alicia knew that Eleanor thought that she was the person for Adam. Unfortunately, the other woman didn't know the reality of the situation. If anything, Adam distrusted Alicia more than any of the women from his past. He thought she'd stolen from him. The other women had tried to cheat him but Adam genuinely thought that Alicia had made a fool of him. That certainly eliminated any possible future for the two of them, not that she'd want one anyway, Alicia told herself.

"I hope he finds that woman," she said and forced herself to look away.

Eleanor wouldn't let the subject drop yet. "You aren't that woman?" she asked softly.

"No. Adam won't ever fall in love with me," Alicia replied, unknowingly revealing the sadness she felt in her heart.

"But that's not true for you, is it?" she asked.

Alicia opened her mouth to reply but no words would form.

Eleanor pulled her sunglasses off and looked intently at Alicia. After a few moments, she seemed to come to some sort of conclusion. "I'm going to tell you something which very few people know. If Adam knew that I were telling you this he'd be very angry but I don't think you're the type of person who would abuse the knowledge."

Alicia felt as if something momentous was going to be imparted and she braced herself. She wasn't sure she wanted to hear whatever Eleanor was going to say. Alicia could feel her stomach muscles clench and her shoulders stiffen. "I'm sure Adam's the typical, poor little rich boy," Alicia tried to dismiss, a smile on her face.

Eleanor shook her head frantically. "No really! That's completely the opposite of Adam. I'm not surprised that you would say that though. He's pretty good at hiding his past."

Alicia swallowed painfully. "What do you mean?" she asked. Half of her told her to get up and run away. A sixth sense told her that whatever Eleanor was going to tell her would be too painful to hear. But another part of her longed to know more about this enigmatic man that had dominated her life, not just for the month she'd been living under his roof but for the past two months, knowing that Adam had occupied her thoughts almost every moment, both sleeping and awake, since that fateful night she'd met him at his company party.

Eleanor looked over at the two men still sparring on the tennis courts. "Adam wasn't brought up in wealth. The complete opposite in fact. His mother was actually a drug addict that lost custody of him when he turned two years old. He grew up in a series of awful foster homes."

Alicia frowned. "I thought Adam went to Oxford for university."

"He did. But that was on scholarship because he really is a genius. His IQ is much higher than the average smart person. I don't know what it is, but he knows more than most people could ever dream of knowing."

"Then, how did he get into Oxford? I thought that school was a haven for the rich and privileged."

Eleanor laughed. "There's no denying that it definitely has a history of taking the crème of British society. But you have to be pretty smart, nevertheless. Otherwise, you'd never make it through the classes. And Adam was at the top of his graduating class."

"Really?" Alicia gasped, impressed despite herself.

"Really," Eleanor confirmed. "But that's not really what makes Adam tick. He's a brilliant businessman and can find profit in just about any endeavor. Your real challenge is going to be his distrust of women."

Alicia had to ask. She knew she shouldn't but the question came out anyway. "Why does he distrust women?"

Eleanor grimaced and Alicia thought she wasn't going to answer her. But then she looked over at the tennis courts one more time. "Because his mother is the worst woman that has ever set face on this earth," she said simply.

Alicia gasped. "The worst?" she laughed but it came out as a squeak instead. "Surely she can't be all that bad," she joked.

Eleanor shook her head. "After Adam made his first million, he was only about twenty-one or twenty-two. The evil woman found him and pretended to be redeemed. She said she wanted to prove to Adam that she could be a good mother to him."

"What did he do?" Alicia asked, knowing the answer even before it was given.

"You mean after Adam took her into his house, fed her, clothed her with beautiful designer clothes? She stole about a hundred thousand dollars, then disappeared." Eleanor bit her lip and shook her head. "What the awful person didn't know was that Adam would have happily given her the money, plus much more. A more generous man I've never known. But what she did hardened Adam towards her. She even bragged about it in some silly rag when she sold her story to it for even more money."

"What happened to her?"

Alicia watched as Eleanor gritted her teeth slightly before answering. "She died about five years ago of a drug overdose. She was broke again, sitting in a hovel with a needle in her arm."

"What did Adam do?" Alicia asked, fighting back the tears. She'd had a horrible childhood as well but at least her mother was around for emotional support at times. And before her father had been imprisoned, they had been an extremely happy family.

"Nothing. He wouldn't even pay for her funeral. She was buried in a pauper's grave. Once Adam dismisses someone from his life, they are completely dead to him."

Alicia wiped a tear from the corner of her eye, hoping Eleanor didn't see the revealing gesture. Meanwhile, her heart was aching for the small boy who had never been hugged or tucked in at night. Had anyone ever sang him songs or helped him with his homework? What about his first date? Who guided him through the mysteries of dating? She looked across the expanse of the pool and soft, green grass to the tennis courts where the men were laughing and wiping their faces with towels.

He was so strong and confident, Alicia had been sure he'd grown up in a privileged house with both parents doting on him. But now she realized that he never received a call from either parent nor did he talk about family members. He was completely alone in the world.

What could she do about it? He distrusted her just as much as he distrusted his mother. Well, maybe not as much since he was willing to keep her in his house and within his sights.

As the two men approached the pool, Alicia considered everything she'd heard. Could she make him see the wonderful side of life? Did she have the courage to show him how to care? She didn't think she did.

"What are you thinking about?" Adam asked, tossing his towel onto her lap and leering at her. "You're looking entirely too serious for a morning spent by the pool doing nothing," he said. He sat down beside her on the lounge chair, forcing her to move her legs out of the way in the nick of time.

"We were coming up with ideas for the evening," Eleanor piped in.

"I'm afraid evening plans are going to be discussed at a later time," Gary said, grabbing his wife's hands and pulling her to a standing position. In a graceful movement, he tossed her over his shoulder, ignoring the yelp his elegant wife let out as he carried her caveman style across the pool patio. "I just couldn't stand to see my lovely wife being so sweet, innocent and dignified. I'm going to have to show her she's a woman and not simply a lady," he laughed.

Within moments, the two had disappeared through the path towards the house. Alicia smothered a laugh when she heard Eleanor's demands of "Put me down, you awful brute," or "You will definitely regret this, Gary!" when he failed to comply with her commands.

Alicia watched them walk away, laughter in her eyes and a wistful expression on her face.

"What were the two of you talking about?" Adam asked, drawing her attention back to him.

Alicia lifted her shoulders gently. "She told me a lot about the history of the house," Alicia said, thinking back to the beginning of the conversation. "She said that this used to be a manor home for a Lord and Lady. Apparently there is still a ghost that roams the hallways?" she smiled, hoping he wouldn't see the omission in her eyes. "Is that true? Have you seen the ghost?"

Adam chuckled. "No ghosts so far," he said. "But I've heard the rumors." He stood up and leered at her. "I think I need to cool down," he said. "And I think you are looking a little hot as well."

Alicia glanced up quickly, saw the look in Adam's eyes and took action swiftly. Unfortunately, she wasn't fast enough and, just as she was pushing out of the chair to the right, opposite Adam, he grabbed her by the waist and lifted her easily into his arms. "Oh, no you don't," he said and walked over to the pool.

"Adam, don't you dare! You're not even dressed in a bathing suit," she squealed. But a moment later, she was taking a deep breath before the water closed over her head. She pushed up from the bottom quickly, sputtering as she surfaced. "I can't believe you did that!" she said, pushing her hair out of her face. "Adam Meyers, you are bad!" she said, splashing him but it was pointless since he was right next to her, completely drenched in water as well.

"I know. But I like being evil with you," he said and put his arms around her water slicked waist.

Alicia eyed his mischievous face warily. "What are you thinking now?" she asked.

Adam shrugged casually but pulled her against his body. "Why would you think I'm planning anything?" he asked.

Alicia laughed, feeling like a teenager again. How she could feel so carefree when she was still his captive and she'd just heard the tragic story of his youth, she didn't understand. She chalked it up to the fact that, being with Adam, she felt more alive than at any other time.

Alicia looked into his eyes, saw the amusement there and knew she was in trouble despite his claims of innocence. "Adam, you're going to do something. What are you thinking?" she demanded, starting to struggle. But it was no use. His arms and stomach were rock solid walls of muscle which made her defenseless against his intentions. She tried to push against his shoulders but there wasn't much strength in her since she was now laughing so hard she could barely breathe.

"Why don't you trust me?"

She only laughed harder. "Trust has never been a factor in this relationship," she gasped and looked behind her. "And now I know that it still shouldn't be!" Alicia understood his intentions only a moment before the waterfall dumped over her head. She laughed so hard she had to gasp for breath but instead of pushing away, she wrapped her arms around his neck and held herself close. If she was going to get doused, so was he.

She heard him chuckle and then felt his body move again, out from under the waterfall. The laughter helped Alicia forget the story she'd just heard. These were not the actions of a man demented from the pain of his mother's abandonment and subsequent betrayal. This was the man she was in love with, she thought. Even more now that she'd heard he wasn't a rich playboy.

The idea made her freeze and she looked up into his eyes.

"What's wrong?" he asked, his arms gentling and he gave her a little more space, but not much.

Alicia's mouth was open and her blue eyes were still looking into his dark, curious ones. She'd have to break away from this emotion she told herself. That path only led to pain and disappointment. She would have to guard her heart against that kind of emotion building up inside her. Adam hated her. He wanted her body but not her love.

"That expression on your face has to go," he said. His hand slipped around her waist but gone was the teasing expression. There was a more intent look on his face.

She swiftly hid her feelings and tried to appear casual. "What kind of expression would you like on it?" she asked, already knowing the answer. And she was there. It seemed that the moment he touched her, she was just as on fire for satisfaction as he was.

Adam looked down into her eyes and noticed the softened expression, the need in her eyes and the slightly opened mouth. "I think you've already gained the right expression. Now we must work on your comments," he commented and slid his hand down to cover her bottom, then moved his hands down over her outer thighs. He gripped her waist and hauled her upwards, pulling her legs around his waist.

"What's wrong with my comments?" she asked, fighting for breath as the excitement of his touch took over her senses.

"A moment ago you were saying 'no Adam' and 'don't do that Adam'. At this moment, I'd prefer 'please don't stop Adam' or 'More Adam'," he said and took her nipple into his mouth.

The heat of his mouth after the cool water of the pool was shocking. She inhaled sharply and her hands gripped his shoulders. She arched her back to give him better access. "Don't stop, Adam!" she called out.

"That's better. How about the other part?"

"More! Please more!"

"Say my name," he ordered softly. His fingers slipped underneath her bathing suit, finding her core and slipping easily inside, moving slowly.

"Adam!" she called out, her body moving restlessly against his.

"That's good," he said but his voice was husky as well and she could feel the reaction of his body.

When he took his hands out suddenly, Alicia's eyes snapped open. "What?" she demanded.

Adam grimaced. "I think I've made a tactical error," he said and moved out through the waterfall to the stairs at the other end of the pool. "But we can remedy that immediately."

"What are you going to do?" she asked, grabbing onto his shoulders as he simply walked out of the pool with her in his arms. He strode across the patio and back down the pathway, not slowing his stride until they were behind the closed doors of his bedroom.

"I don't think your housekeeper will like the fact that we've splattered water all over the house," she said as he walked to the bathroom.

"I don't give a damn about the housekeeper right at this moment. I care about getting you naked and having you say those things again," he said, letting her slide down his body.

Alicia complied quickly, watching as he pulled off his drenched tennis clothes.

Moments later, wrapped in a towel and completely dry again except for her hair, Alicia was picked up and carried over to the bed.

"Okay, lady, say the words," he said, his mouth covering her nipple yet again.

Alicia needed no more encouragement. Her fingers tangled in his damp hair, holding his head close and her body writhing under his. "More," she whispered, almost unable to say the words as his fingers moved down her body, his body filling hers as he moved to an ancient rhythm.

The release Alicia felt was nothing less than earth shattering. She cried out, holding onto Adam as she climaxed, her body wrapped around his in any way it could.

As her body floated back to reality, her arms relaxed and she stared up at Adam, embarrassed for the first time about her reaction to him. He looked back at her, a smile on his face as he gave her a tender kiss.

Then he quickly pulled away and walked into the shower, leaving Alicia to wonder if she'd actually experienced that moment of tenderness or if she had only imagined it. She heard the shower start and sighed deeply.

What had happened this afternoon? Why had this time with

Adam been so much more intense than the other times? She'd thought that nothing could make the orgasms between the two of them stronger but she'd been wrong. This time had actually been mind-blowing.

Alicia pulled the towel back around her, feeling abandoned and wishing she could ignore that feeling. Adam was giving her all that he wanted to give her. And she would have to be satisfied with that.

Besides, she wasn't in this relationship for herself. She'd actually forgotten that over the past week. Where had the resentment gone? Why wasn't she feeling trapped and caged in any longer?

Alicia grimaced as she stood up. She'd been with Adam for a little more than six weeks and she was actually feeling....happy?

She shook her head, denying that happiness was her current reality. No, she was just drifting on a cloud of really good sex. That was all.

But then Adam walked back into the room and all her feelings of contentment splintered with his words. He was wearing silk boxers already but nothing else. "You really should get a move on. Rosa probably has appetizers ready." He pulled on a pair of black, casual slacks and a white shirt, leaving the collar casually unbuttoned.

"What is on the agenda?"

He grinned wolfishly. "A casual dinner, then back up here for more of the same." He walked over to tower above her. "Does that sound like it would satisfy all of your desires?" he asked.

Alicia looked deeply into his eyes, wondering why her heart was actually hurting with his words. But she forced a smile to form on her lips and shrugged. "Only if you're up to it," she said suggestively. The moment of sophistication was spoiled when her face flamed with embarrassed color.

Adam caught the blush and laughed, pulling her into his arms and kissing the top of her head. "I love the effort but I don't think you're ready to play the siren yet."

He patted her bottom before heading for the door. "Come on downstairs when you're ready."

Alicia glared at the closed door, wishing she could just dive into the bed and hide under the covers. When would she stop trying to beat him at his own game? He was the expert and she should just accept that.

But she couldn't, she thought as she headed for the shower herself. And what was worse, she wanted more from him than just casual sex. Where that had come from, she had no idea, but as she lathered her hair and rinsed, she knew that the feelings were true.

What was she going to do about them was the next question. She pulled another towel from the stack beside the shower area. Dressing was easy now that she had a fancy new wardrobe. She pulled on a pretty yellow sundress that made her skin look softer and creamy. Brushing her hair, she decided to just leave it down but pull it back with a clip on the top so it would stay out of her eyes during dinner.

She applied some mascara and lipstick and considered herself presentable. Standing up, she surveyed her appearance in the mirror. The sundress hugged her breasts and waist gently then flared out around her hips, making her waist look smaller and her breasts look larger. The design was amazingly flattering and she had to acknowledge that the expensive dress was a masterpiece. She felt pretty and desirable. Would Adam agree? Would he resent the amount she'd spent on the dress?

She hated being insecure about how much of his money she'd spent. He was the one who had sent her to the expensive store. So if he didn't like it, he could just rot, she told herself and swung around to head out of the bedroom.

As soon as she walked down the stone stairway, she heard the laughter. Apparently, she was the last one to change and come downstairs.

"Good evening," Adam called, walking over to her as soon as she appeared. He took her hand and led her into the room, pouring her a glass of something yellow that was in a pitcher on the bar. "I hope you like it," he said, handing her the liquid in an interesting martini type of glass. "Rosa discovered the drink in a romance novel a few weeks ago and has been eager to try it out on her guinea pigs," he explained.

Alicia eyed the liquid suspiciously. "In a romance novel?" she asked, wary immediately.

"Of course," Eleanor said, raising her glass to clink the edge of Alicia's gently. "Something about Brazil and lemons. I wasn't sure about the rest of what she said but apparently Adam was fine with her explanation."

Alicia looked to Adam for an explanation but he only raised one eyebrow, as if daring her to take a sip. Alicia of course, could never back down from a challenge so she tasted the icy liquid and found it to be amazingly sweet and wonderful. "It's delicious," she said, taking a longer sip.

"I thought you'd like it," he said, lifting his glass of bourbon to his lips.

"You're not drinking Rosa's concoction?" she asked, raising her eyebrow just as he had done a moment ago.

"I don't think so," he replied evenly, amusement erupting from his expression.

"Why not? Too girly for you? Are you afraid of testing your masculinity? Might be challenged, huh?" she asked and turned around.

She had her back to him but she already knew that he wouldn't allow her to get away with such a comment. She almost laughed out loud when she was smacked on the bottom. She turned around and glared instead.

"I don't think you want to challenge my masculinity, do you?" he asked, one hand moving to clasp her wrist in his, while his thumb rested alongside her pulse. "I think I could do a very good job of proving myself to you."

Alicia shook her head mutely.

Adam chuckled. "No, I didn't think so."

Gary laughed at that point as well. "Now that my friend's manliness is satisfied, how about a friendly game of pool?" he asked. "Don't you have a pool table around this mausoleum somewhere?"

Alicia glanced at Adam who only nodded. "Absolutely. It is down the hallway."

Gary simply laughed and thwacked Adam on the back. Turning to his wife he said, "That look means that he knows he can beat me yet again but he's being too polite to say so in front of my lady love," he explained, humor in his eyes. Turning back to Adam he shook his head as he said, "Dear boy, you have to have a weakness somewhere. And I'm determined to find it."

"I'm not the best at pool," Adam said politely.

Gary only shook his head in mock misery. Looking at Alicia he said, "That translates into, 'I'm pretty good but I'm too polite to tell you not to challenge me,'" he explained. "But you know what, old man?" Gary rallied gamely, "I'm going to do it anyway. I'll have these lovely ladies on my side to cheer me on," he said.

"Cheer you on?" Alicia said. "Are the ladies not allowed to participate?" she asked, rising to the bait.

Gary was instantly interested. "Are you saying that you'd like to play?"

Eleanor shook her head, laughing hilariously. "Don't do it, Alicia. These men have competition down to a blood sport," she cautioned.

Alicia looked over at Adam and considered his expression. She'd spent many years playing pool as she bartended in both high school and college, whiling away the hours when she didn't have customers. It hadn't been one of the hard core, biker area pool halls, just a nice hamburger joint that also had pool tables in the back for the non-eating, beer drinking customers.

"I might not win," she lied smoothly, trying to ease them into a false sense of security until she could gauge their expertise against her own. "But I can probably hold my own," she said.

Two hours later, she chalked her pool stick and then set up her angle, gauging the distance and the timing. Taking a shot, she knocked the last two balls into the hole then turned to face the gentlemen who were sitting on the sidelines sipping their drinks in stunned silence. Eleanor was the only one making any noise and she was bouncing on the bar stool, clapping her hands in her appreciation for Alicia's expertise.

She hopped down and took Alicia's pool stick in her hands, placing it back into the holder. "Well, that was an invigorating game, wasn't it gentlemen?" she asked, slipping her arm through Alicia's. "I can't tell you when I've enjoyed watching pool more than tonight. And now," she said, with humor in her eyes, "I think it is time for dinner."

Gary and Eleanor left Sunday afternoon and Alicia was genuinely sorry to see them go. They were nice people and she'd felt as if she and Eleanor were friends. It had been a long time since she'd had a friend other than a co-worker.

Alicia and Adam were standing out on the front steps, waving to the couple as they drove off and Alicia felt awkward since the scene was more reminiscent of a married couple than of her true relationship with Adam. She didn't want him to think she was assuming anything. But she was feeling depressed now that they were gone. Would Adam start ignoring her again and turning to her only when he wanted sex? The thought sent a chill through her bones and she wrapped her arms around her middle.

"What's wrong?" Adam asked, putting an arm around her waist.

Not wanting him to misinterpret anything, she forced a smile on her face. "Nothing. It was a nice weekend. Thank you for letting me come along and get to know your friends."

"They liked you too."

She looked at the buttons on his shirt front before continuing, knowing she wouldn't be able to hide her laughter. "I guess they won't know they were robbed blind until they get home, huh?"

Adam pulled back suddenly, his eyes searching hers but at that point, she could no longer hold back her laughter. "You're teasing?" he demanded. When she laughed harder and tried to take a step backwards, he shook his head. "Oh, no you don't!" He tossed her over his shoulder as if she were a sack of flour and walked back into the house.

"What are you doing?" she demanded, putting a hand on his back and trying to see through her hair which was now covering her face. But she couldn't stop laughing enough to put any force into her words. "Adam, put me down," she demanded between gasps of laughter.

His only response was to smack her bottom playfully.

When she realized he was heading back upstairs, her laughter only increased. "What? Are you going to punish me by making me go back to sleep?" she challenged.

"Oh, you're going to beg for mercy by the time I'm done with you but you won't get it."

The door closed and the next thing she knew, she was being tossed onto her back on the bed with Adam's body covering her own.

Making love to Adam with laughter was a wonderful experience, she thought an hour later as she pulled on a pair of shorts. Adam was going to teach her to play tennis and she knew she wouldn't be much of a challenge to him on the courts. But she was excited anyway.

This whole weekend had given her hope that Adam might start thinking of her as something other than a convenient sexual partner or a crook.

Her hands stilled on the button to her shorts. Why would it matter that he was thinking of her differently, she asked herself. Why should she care? She wasn't anything to him and as soon as he'd determined that she had paid off whatever someone else had stolen, he would move on.

She bit her lower lip, considering everything that had happened over the past several weeks. Adam had changed, especially this weekend, she thought.

Pulling on a tee-shirt, she considered her options. She could simply push these feelings down into herself, ignore them and hope that, when the relationship ended, she would be able to go her own way. Or she could fight for him, show him that he needed her in his life. And he did, she knew. Adam was happier, lighter, more relaxed. She'd seen it this weekend. Had it only been because he was around his friends? Or could it be that he'd enjoyed her company as much as she'd enjoyed his?

The fact that he was willing to spend Sunday with her alone, teaching her to play tennis, and not rushing back to the city and his work, gave her hope. He might not have feelings for her, but he wasn't pushing her into a small section of his life and ordering her about anymore.

Could she let that hope flourish? Was it wise?

Probably not, she accepted. But there was nothing she could do about it. Despite her father's actions that had left her mother and sister in a painful situation, Alicia was basically an optimist. Otherwise, she'd never have been able to survive her high school and college years, supporting her family through that painful period. After her father had died, it had been so much better and everyone's spirits had lifted, including hers.

Pulling on an old pair of sneakers, she tied the laces and made up her mind. She'd fought so hard for her family, working menial jobs that had put food on the table and paid off the mortgage. She'd been fighting for her family's survival for so long, it was time for her to start thinking about herself.

And if it didn't work out, if she discovered that Adam couldn't return her love or even start to care for her, then she would deal with that later. Meanwhile, she had an undiscovered time with him and she would use it to make him start to care for her. She wasn't sure exactly how she would do it but at a minimum, she would put a little bit of fun into his life.

How much time did she have with him? She'd have to ask that question, knowing it would only remind him of her assumed perfidy but that couldn't be helped. She would need all the data in order to form her plan.

Feeling better, she left his bedroom and skipped down the stairs. He was waiting at the bottom, two tennis racquets in one hand while he watched the stairs.

"It's about time," he said, his eyes never leaving her as she walked down the stairs.

"Sorry, I didn't know you were waiting for me. I thought you'd gone over to the courts already."

"Nope. But I told Rosa that we'd go out to dinner instead of eating in if that's okay with you. She apparently has something she wanted to attend tonight."

"That sounds very nice. Her granddaughter is singing in a play tonight," Alicia explained.

They were walking out of the house and down the pathway towards the tennis courts. "How do you know that?"

Alicia looked back at him, surprised at the question. "I asked her," Alicia said simply.

"When?"

Alicia considered taking offense at his snappy question but she looked at him and he only looked curious, not suspicious. "Last night when she was serving the meal. You were talking to Gary about some sort of rumor that had been spreading throughout the industry. Eleanor asked Rosa about where she'd learned to cook. She told us about her grandchildren and that's when she mentioned that her granddaughter was singing in the choir tonight."

"Why didn't she tell me?" he asked, moving forward to walk on ahead.

Alicia raised one shoulder. "Possibly because you were engrossed in a conversation."

Adam looked back at Alicia, wondering how she was able to draw out people so often. It didn't matter what socio-economic status they held, she was open and friendly with everyone. Was that part of the way she gained people's trust and had avoided prosecution so far? How much had she stolen from others?

But as he watched her walk along side him, he knew that his convictions about her character just didn't fit any longer. There was the one side that was the criminal and he had an entire file folder full of proof of that. But something niggled at him.

He pushed those thoughts aside, preferring to deal with the here and now. And right now, she was looking incredibly sexy in a pair of khaki shorts that had definitely seen better days and an old tee-shirt that had a hole in the side. "I thought you'd bought new clothes," he commented as he set up the automatic ball machine.

"I did," she said, taking the smaller racquet in her hands and feeling the weight.

"You didn't get new shorts," he pointed out.

Alicia laughed. "Of course I did. But what's wrong with these? Eleanor and Gary aren't around so I didn't think it would be necessary to wear something nicer."

Adam didn't say anything but his mind automatically thought back to other women he'd been with in the past. They had spent his money as if it were theirs, constantly needing one more thing to make whatever ensemble they were considering work better or match more perfectly. And here was a woman who had stolen over one hundred thousand dollars from him and yet she didn't even bother buying decent clothes. What had she spent all the money on?

Adam realized there was more to this situation than he had realized. Loose ends bothered him as did unanswered questions. He was going to have to get Jim to look into her finances a little more carefully.

He set the tennis ball machine to slow and then walked Alicia through the various serves and volleys. After an hour, he had to admit, she had the potential for being a decent player.

They finished the lesson and Alicia walked off, allowing Adam a chance to work out a little more hardily with the machine while she changed into her suit for a swim. The afternoon turned out to be wonderfully relaxing. She pulled a book off of his shelf and carried it with her to the pool. Then she spent the afternoon watching Adam play tennis against himself, noting that he was just as ferocious against a machine as he was against Gary. He then changed and joined her by the pool, reading through several papers he'd brought down. They swam and Adam worked, eventually Alicia dozed off, exhausted after the evening with

Adam in which she hadn't gotten much sleep since he'd made love to her twice. The man's sexual appetite was truly amazing, she thought as she closed her eyes. But then, so was hers where he was concerned.

He took her to a lovely restaurant for dinner and she wore her last cocktail dress, feeling extremely special walking next to Adam who was dressed in a sharp suit with a maroon tie. Dressing for their evening had been another odd experience where she'd started to feel married to him. It had been a very intimate period and she was savoring the moments with him as long as she had him near.

The food was delicious and Adam shared more stories of his college years with her, making her laugh and feel extraordinarily special.

Dancing in his arms to the soft music made her feel as if she were on a cloud. She laid her head on his shoulder and pretended that no one else was around. She loved hearing his strong heartbeat and feeling his muscles as they wrapped around her. He was so gentle, she thought but had so much power behind his amazing body.

"Having a romantic time?" a harsh male voice asked from behind her.

Alicia instantly stiffened and she felt Adam's body do the same. Obviously Adam didn't like the man either.

"Evening, Roger. What can I do for you?" Adam asked the man.

Alicia turned to face the man, assuming it was the polite thing to do. But as soon as she turned, she felt the man's eyes slide down her figure. The man practically undressed her, leering as he did so. Alicia felt so uncomfortable, she unconsciously moved closer to Adam and felt better when he put his arm around her waist, pulling her even closer to his strength.

"How about a dance with this little lady? I haven't seen her around lately. A new mare for your stables?" he asked crudely.

Alicia was so horrified by the man's comments she couldn't hold back her gasp. Adam didn't like his insinuations either and pulled her close, his body turning to shield her from the man's disgusting behavior.

"If you'll excuse us, Roger," Adam said and Alicia could feel the bunched muscles underneath the sophisticated veneer of his tailored suit.

"You? Of course, but maybe the lady would like to speak for herself? How about it, doll?" he asked and moved closer, trying to see around Adam's large body.

"I don't think so," Alicia said as politely as possible under the circumstances.

They walked back to the table and Alicia was finally able to get Adam to smile again although it took all of her conversational skills.

"Let's get out of here," he said, taking her hand and kissing the ends of her fingers. If she had any doubt in her mind why he wanted to leave, it was eliminated with his actions.

"Absolutely. Let me just go to the ladies room," she said, her eyes already moving over him as if she was ready to be with him, alone.

"I'll meet you out front in a few minutes," he said and signaled to the waiter for the check.

Alicia walked through the restaurant and lobby with a silly, romantic grin on her face. In the bathroom, she looked at her appearance and was shocked at the transformation. It wasn't just the dress. Her lipstick was gone but her lips were still red, her cheeks rosy and there was a starry eyed look on her face that probably told the whole world that she was in love with Adam.

Splashing water on her hands and neck, she tried to cool down her racing pulse but it was no use. She had been with Adam for several weeks now and knew exactly what he was capable of as soon as the bedroom door was closed behind them. She should be ashamed and if her mother or sister ever found out that she was no better than a rich man's mistress, she would be. But right now, with the promise of Adam's lovemaking to guide her into the night, she couldn't care less.

Stepping out of the ladies room, she was glancing down at her appearance to make sure everything was in place. If she'd been looking up, she never would have run into the large, obese man but since she hadn't been paying attention, the man caught her off guard.

109

"Well, well, what have we here?" Roger's deep, raspy voice said.

Alicia almost gagged at the pungent smell of a recently smoked cigarette on his clothes. His breath was even worse since the man had eaten something that made him simply reek of onions. The two smells together were too much and she pushed back on his shoulders, her face turned away and a grimace on her face.

"Let me go!" she demanded through gritted teeth.

"Why should I?" he asked, one hand coming up to grip her hair painfully.

"Because I asked you to and this is a public place," Alicia articulated as quickly as she could, so she could stop breathing in the awful smell of the man. She realized the sickly smell of sweat and stench on him too.

"Don't be shy, little dove. If you're nice to me, I can guarantee that I'll be much more generous that your boring, workaholic Adam Meyers. I'm more into the fulfillment of the flesh rather than the chase of the next business deal."

"No thank you," she said, starting to panic. The man was large but had a great deal of muscle underneath his flab. "Please let me go," she said, leaning as far back as she possibly could. Unfortunately, they were in a small area that was hidden from others by both dim lighting as well as strategic walls.

The man smiled grotesquely. "You like to fight, eh? Well, don't worry about that. I like it when women play hard to get. And I show them how to play it better than most," he laughed.

"Uh!" Alicia said, grimacing as the man's beefy hand moved up to touch her cheek. "Let me go!" she cried out. "You're disgusting and I'd never even consider you for a dance partner much less a boyfriend!" she said, knowing it wasn't tactful but she didn't care anymore. She was gagging over the man's smell as well as his touch which was making her skin crawl.

When something tore, she didn't really think about it, too desperate to get out of his hands.

Suddenly, she was free and stumbling backwards. Opening her eyes, she saw that Adam was holding Roger by the lapels of his suit coat, a look of rage crossing his face.

She could see that he was going to do something he'd regret in the morning so she put a soft hand on his shoulder. Instantly, she felt his muscles relax slightly but he was still right on the edge of fury.

"Don't ever touch her again," Adam said to the now red faced man.

Adam released him and turned to Alicia. "Are you okay?" he asked, taking her gently into his arms.

"Yes. I think so," she said, then gasped when she realized that her dress was torn off her shoulder. "Oh, Adam! The dress is torn," she said and the tears started falling.

Roger just didn't know when to stop. "Don't be a fool, Adam," he said, almost swaggering. "She was begging for me. Let her go and go find yourself someone who isn't such a tramp. This one likes it rough and I know how to treat someone like that," he said, licking his lips in anticipation.

She felt his muscles tense but didn't have a chance to stop him since she was too shocked by the obscene man's words. Adam set her gently away from him and then in one, deft movement, he slammed his fist into the fat Roger's jaw. The man toppled like a lead weight.

Adam then took Alicia into his arms, swinging her legs up and cradled her as he snapped at the doorman to open the door. Thankfully, Adam's Jaguar was already waiting at the bottom of the stone stairs and he placed her into the seat before rushing around to the other side of the car.

On the ride home, the shaking started and she huddled into a mass of fear and anger in the corner of the leather seat.

When they arrived at the house, Adam strode over to the side of the car and lifted her up in his arms, carrying her up to the bedroom they'd shared for the past three days.

"I'm sorry," Adam said. "I didn't know he would be waiting in ambush for you." He placed her gently in one of the overstuffed chairs that was sitting by the dark fireplace before striding over to a small table and poured her a large snifter of brandy. "Are you going to be okay?" he asked, kneeling in front of her, his dark eyes looking worriedly at her face as if the signs for her reaction would be written there for him.

"Yes. I'll be fine," she said, accepting the glass of brandy even though she didn't really want it. What she wanted was for Adam to pull her into his arms and hold her, push away the bad feelings and replace them with good ones. But he didn't look like he was willing to do that. He looked angry and she watched as a muscle twitched in his jaw. "Why in the world would you maintain a friendship with someone like him?" she asked, worried that the question would spur more anger but needing to know the answer.

Adam's eyes sharpened but he shook his head. "Roger isn't my friend in any sense of the word. In fact, he's one of those revolting human beings that leech off the rest of the world. I have only contempt for him."

Alicia shivered and took a tentative sip of the brandy, as much for something to do rather than needing the liquid. She coughed as the liquid burned her throat but a moment later, she actually felt slightly better. The warmth soothed her from the inside. It still wasn't what she needed though. "I guess you do business with him?"

Adam turned his back to her and shook his head again. "No, the opposite, in fact."

That comment made her curious and when she accepted that he wasn't going to elaborate, she asked him the question, "What do you mean?"

Adam took a deep breath and faced her again, his face grim. "I actually made him go out of business. It wasn't an intentional situation, but if I had it to do over again, I'd make sure I ruined the man. He was able to bail on the company his family left to him with enough to last him a lifetime."

"Ah. Well that explains his animosity and his need to denigrate anything that is yours."

Adam stiffened and looked at her intently. "Are you saying that you're mine, Alicia?" he asked softly.

Her hand froze and she looked back at him. He seemed nervous about her answer, as if it meant a great deal to him. But what was the right answer? Did he want her to be his in more than just a financial sense? That was ridiculous. That would mean he already felt something for her other than simple lust. She was just looking for things that she wanted to see instead of what was really there, she told herself.

"I'm here with you now, aren't I?" she said simply. "But you have to make tonight better," she said, putting the brandy aside and standing up. "You brought me there, you're going to have to fix it," she said, a little unsteadily.

Adam's shoulders were tense but he turned to face her. "What can I do to make it up to you?" he asked. "A diamond bracelet?" he suggested. "Perhaps a trip to Europe? One of the hot spots, perhaps?"

Alicia looked at him, confused. "No. None of that will work."

Adam sighed. "Alicia, you're going to have to spell it out for me. I'm not a mind reader," he said harshly.

She stood there, feeling scared and vulnerable but said the words anyway, terrified that he would reject her and turn away from her. If he did, so be it, she thought. "I need you to hold me. I need you to put your arms around me and make me feel clean again," she said.

His eyes showed his surprise. "That's what will fix this?" he asked, stunned.

"Yes," she said and her voice broke on the word. She was shaking again, needing to feel his warmth and strength and scared that he was going to turn away from her. He had every right to. It wasn't his responsibility but she desperately needed him right now.

He didn't disappoint her. He took her into his arms gently and pulled her close, his hands enfolding her into his strength. For a long time, he simply held her, his hands rubbing her back and shoulders gently. But when she lifted her head from his shoulder, she told him without words that this was not enough. She slipped her hands higher and wrapped them around his neck, pulling his face closer to hers so she could kiss him.

For the rest of the night, she felt loved and secure. She knew that in the morning, they would drive back to New York and he would leave her at the door just as he always did but for tonight, she was in his arms and he was being amazingly tender and caring. His loving yet again was different and more fulfilling. She cried out her release, holding him close as the waves crashed over her again and again.

Chapter 9

Alicia smiled and rolled over onto her stomach. She loved listening as Adam showered and shaved for the day. He always woke up before her but she had no idea how he did it. He had no alarm and the sun still wasn't over the horizon. The man was part machine, she was sure of it.

Her smile grew as she realized what she had been thinking. He definitely wasn't completely a machine, she thought. Every night for the past week, he had been a completely different person. It was as if their weekend together had changed something in their relationship. He still joked about her theft but he didn't seem serious about it anymore. And he was caring and gentle, loving almost.

The shower stopped and Alicia pulled herself up, then slipped out of bed, pulling on the gorgeous silk robe Adam had sent to her one day earlier. That was another thing. Boxes of clothes arrived daily. Sometimes there were several boxes filled with the most beautiful clothes. Other times it was only a simple scarf or something sweet like chocolate covered cherries. Wednesday it had been a box of chocolates. Thursday it had been a stunning evening gown. She had no idea when she would wear something so beautiful but maybe Adam had an excursion already planned. Now it was Friday and she wondered what the weekend could hold. Before the weekend in Martha's Vineyard, Adam had spent most weekends working so Alicia could barely differentiate between the weekdays and the weekends, they all had the same pattern.

Tying the sash around her slim waist, she padded barefoot into the bathroom. Leaning against the door frame, she watched as Adam shaved, only a towel around his waist so she had a full view of his impressive muscles.

His eyes roved over her silk clad figure and his hand froze midway between the running water and his shaving cream covered face. "If you continue to stand there looking incredibly sexy like that, don't be surprised if you find yourself right back in bed, minus that robe," he growled, his dark eyes intense as he looked at her in the mirror.

Alicia smiled, not taking him seriously since she knew he was on his way to work. Besides, he'd made love to her quite thoroughly just the previous evening. "How do you wake up so early every morning?" she asked, walking over to lean against the counter to look up at him directly instead of through the mirror.

Adam looked down into her lovely face, noting with satisfaction the tumbled hair and the slightly swollen lips. He'd put that look of satisfaction on her face, he knew. And he liked seeing her in the nice clothes. She needed more of them, he thought. A pang of guilt pushed itself into his thoughts but he pushed it aside. He'd already asked Jim to look over the evidence again. Too many points just didn't add up, most importantly, the fact that Alicia just didn't seem like a thief to him. She seemed sweet and innocent, just like the image she presented to the world.

He knew all too well that looks could be deceiving so he didn't bring up the fact that he was looking into the evidence again. Because if it came back that she really was the culprit, he wasn't sure what he was going to do with her.

He knew what he wanted to do with her. But he wasn't exactly sure how to go about it. He wanted her to stay in his life forever. It was such an odd feeling, to want to share his life with someone, to talk with them and sit with them at meals and come home at night and know that she will be there. Hell, who was he kidding? He wanted to marry the woman. He wanted to shower her with everything money could buy and keep her in a lifestyle that wouldn't tempt her to steal anything again. But if he'd been wrong all along, and she hadn't stolen the money from him, where would that leave them?

Was he making too much of things? Was she just an extremely good actress? He'd find out soon enough. But in the meantime, he thought, looking down at her nipples pressing against the soft silk fabric.

116

He snapped out of his suppositions, pushing them aside until all the facts were verified and categorized in his mind. Refocusing on her lovely face and easy smile, he said, "How do I wake up?" he repeated, putting down his razor but his face was still half covered with shaving cream. "I have a sexy body pressed against mine and it drives me to the point of waking up."

Alicia rolled her eyes. "No, seriously," she said, slipping up onto the counter, her eyes still slightly sleepy.

Adam shook his head, "You think I'm kidding?" he challenged, then pulled her closer, hearing her gasp as her soft body came into contact with his very hard one. "I guarantee that I am very, very serious," he said, nibbling on her neck and hearing a giggle as she got her face covered with shaving cream.

"Adam, you're going to get that stuff all over me!" she said, wriggling in an effort to get away from him.

"That's not a bad idea," he growled.

Alicia held onto his shoulders, the laughter gone as his hands moved inside her robe, parting the soft folds as his hand covered her breast. Her head fell backwards and her body arched into his, her legs opening and wrapping around his waist. "Adam!" she called out.

His already hard body slipped inside her wet one, her body adjusting instantly to his size as he moved, his hands holding her hips, lifting her up hard against his body as his took over the ancient rhythm. His hand slipped between their bodies, his fingers working magic and within moments, she was crying out her release and Adam followed shortly afterwards with his own.

"Now that's a great way to wake up," he groaned, his mouth sliding against her neck and his hand moving up to cup her breasts.

Her head dropped back against his arm as her body worked its way out of its languor. "I agree," she laughed softly.

She slipped into the shower while he finished shaving. While Adam got dressed, she moved into the kitchen and made him a cup of coffee which he gratefully accepted before passionately kissing her good-bye for the day.

Alicia smiled sadly as the door closed behind him. She had the whole day ahead of her and she wasn't sure exactly what she was going to do to fill it.

Her book! She would continue to write and find out if she had it in her to complete the task. She quickly dressed in a pair of shorts and casual shirt, then turned on her computer. The words seemed to jump out of her fingers as they whipped across the keyboard. It was almost noon before she realized that she hadn't even stopped for breakfast. She was now starving and wandered into the kitchen to find something for lunch. She quickly made herself a sandwich and poured herself a glass of milk, then carried both along with her laptop onto the terrace. The sun was hot but it felt good after the cool of the air-conditioned penthouse. It was also noisier so she could work a little better with the white noise behind her.

The sun was setting when she came out of her work. She was thrilled to see that she'd written about twenty pages. Shutting down the computer, she turned around and stopped short. There was Adam watching her with a strange look on his face.

"What are you doing?" he asked.

Alicia closed her computer quickly, embarrassed about her novice enterprise. "Nothing," she said. "Just surfing the internet," she said. "You have a great wireless network that even reaches out here," she said.

Adam looked across the expanse of the garden terrace. She was lying. For the first time since they'd been together, he was absolutely sure that she was lying. First of all, the wireless network was protected by a security code that only he knew about. He would have gladly given it to her if she'd wanted to surf the internet but that wasn't what she was doing. He knew it deep in his bones.

So what was she doing? He wasn't sure, but he'd damned well find out. There was no way he'd allow her to steal anything else. He ignored the deep stabbing pain that surfaced at the realization that she really was lying to him. After everything they'd shared, she was a cheat, a thief and a liar.

He looked at her, her breasts pushing against the short tank top and cute shorts. He wanted her, regardless of her lack of morals. That was for sure.

First thing this morning, he'd told Jim to go over all the details again and find out what was missing. He explained the areas that didn't seem to add up anymore. But now, he wasn't so sure. Having caught her in a lie, were all the others lies as well?

"Let's go out to dinner," he said and turned away, not even bothering to see if she followed him.

He moved into the bedroom and changed into a pair of black, casual slacks and a white polo shirt, not even glancing her way when she walked in and changed into a bright, yellow sundress.

Alicia wished he would talk to her. She could tell he was angry but she didn't agree that he had any right to be angry with her. She might be his mistress for however long he told her she had to be, but she still had the right to some small amount of privacy. She wasn't going to give in on this issue. He could be mad all he wanted but she wasn't going to tell him what she was doing.

The evening was tense and mostly silent, both Alicia and Adam brewing with their own thoughts. They ate at an Italian restaurant that served excellent pasta that no woman on a diet would ever even breathe inside of for fear of absorbing the calories. The wine was perfect, crisp and clean and a wonderful match with the creamy, cheese laden pasta. They spoke in generalities, Alicia asking him how his day went or if he'd had a lot of meetings. When she only received one word responses, she gave up and ignored him, sipping her wine and pretending to enjoy her meal.

They walked back to the penthouse, Alicia crossing her arms over her chest so he couldn't even try to hold her hand as he had been doing recently. She was too hurt and angry with him to allow him to touch her.

By the time they arrived back at the penthouse, she was furious with him. She wasn't doing anything wrong but he was treating her like she'd just ripped his guts out.

"What's wrong with you?" she demanded, her hands on her hips as she turned and faced him. "You're in an awful mood and I don't think I deserve it."

Adam tossed his keys onto a side table but didn't respond. He walked into his office and quietly closed the door.

From past experience, Alicia knew that he'd be in there for hours. It was only nine o'clock and she didn't want to go to bed just yet. She considered watching television but she'd been out of it for so long, she wasn't sure what the shows were about anymore. She could make some cookies, but that might make him think she was trying to bribe him into a good mood so she discarded that idea as well.

She wanted to pull out her computer and write some more. But could she? Alicia stared at the empty hallway that led to his office. A part of her wanted to storm into his office and get things out into the open. But the other part of her was intimidated by his silent anger.

Defiantly, she picked up her laptop and curled up onto the cozy sofa. She was his mistress. Not his servant or his slave. If he was going to ignore her, then so be it. But she wasn't going to lose this time and be unproductive. Not with so many ideas flying around in her mind.

Alicia stared at the words she'd been writing earlier in the day, trying to gather her thoughts again. As soon as she got into the groove, the words came again, flying out of her mind, through her fingers and into the computer. She actually laughed at some of the dialogue as the hero and heroine were torn apart by the evil villain, who amazingly had similar character traits to Adam at the moment.

By midnight, she considered going to bed but didn't want to stop writing. She'd just rest her head for a few moments, she told herself and put her head onto the cushion behind her. Within moments, she was asleep.

Adam walked into the bedroom, determined to ignore Alicia. He was still furious with her betrayal and wanted to yell and scream at her, to possess her and drive away the need to steal and cheat.

But he stopped short when he saw the empty bed. His temper,

which was already at a slow boil because of her betrayal, moved into explosive. How dare she not be here waiting for him! This was her place. He'd made a deal with her and if she tried to get away from it, he'd have her locked up in jail faster than she could say, "Innocent".

He stormed out of the bedroom, intent on driving over to her old apartment to find her. If she wasn't there....Adam stopped, dead in his tracks when he saw her on the sofa. Her hair was draped across the overstuffed cushions and her hands were limp but laying where they had been poised over the computer keyboard.

The relief that surged through is body at the sight of her made him weak. But he grimly pushed that aside. He wasn't going to let her control him, he told himself. She wasn't worthy of his anxiety or his anger. She was a possession, he reminded himself. Nothing more than a thief working out her prison term. An incredibly beautiful and sexy thief. But nothing more than that.

He walked over to stand above her, his mind working on what he was going to do with her. He should just leave her here. It didn't look like she was very comfortable. And it was late. He should leave her, but he couldn't do it. He walked around to pull the computer away but his eyes caught on the words on the screen. What was she writing? This definitely wasn't the internet, he told himself. He pressed a few more keys and he realized that she didn't even have an internet driver. So there was no way she could be stealing anything from him. She couldn't even check e-mail.

What was she doing? He closed the connections and looked at the screen that was now filled with words. The first line caught his eye and he was intrigued. He pressed a few buttons and the cursor popped to the top of the screen. He sat down next to her, placing the laptop on his knee as he read through the words, captured by the story line already. There were some typos but for a first draft, the mystery was very good. Two hours later, he came to the bottom of the manuscript. A part of him wanted to wake her up and ask her what the next scene would do. He was so caught up in the story he wanted to know how it would end. Another part of him wanted to pull her into his arms and make love to her, more intrigued by the woman he was slowly getting to know. Who was she? This was yet another layer of her personality he'd never suspected.

But what were his suspicions? Adam leaned his head back

against the pillows of the sofa and stared at the ceiling for a long moment. The woman sleeping beside him was a complete mystery and, just like the story she was writing, he wanted to know every detail.

With a deep sigh, he shut down her computer, careful to save the document. He then bent down and picked her up, glad when she automatically curled up into his arms. She trusted him so completely. Why was it so hard for him to trust her?

He was almost to the bedroom when the realization hit him. He did trust her. That was why he'd asked Jim to re-open the investigation and find out who really had perpetuated the embezzlement.

In fact, he loved her. That was why he'd been so upset this evening when she'd lied to him. But he hadn't kicked her out, knowing that it was only a small lie. Unfortunately, any lie between the two of them hurt him more. It was all because of love.

The knowledge freed him in some sort of odd way. He looked down at her, noting the long lashes that lay against her soft, creamy skin. Could she ever love him in return?

He smiled. She already did. He knew that in some deep, elemental way. In fact, she'd probably loved him from the start.

Well, not the beginning, he grimaced and started moving towards the bedroom again. He'd been her first lover and that was probably only curiosity.

And definitely not the second time, since he was accusing her of stealing hundreds of thousands of dollars, threatening imprisonment and fired her on the spot.

He pulled back the covers to the bed and looked at her. Considering all the reasons why she shouldn't care for him, it was actually a miracle that she did. He smiled ruefully, wondering why he hadn't realized both his feelings and her own sooner.

Well, that was all in the past now. It was time to make a clean start. He'd figure out a way to coax her into admitting her feelings for him tomorrow. Adam pulled off her shorts and socks, then undressed himself. Getting into bed next to her, he pulled her into his arms, content to simply hold her. He fell asleep thinking of several ways he'd get her to admit her feelings for him, all of them ending with the two of them making love.

Chapter 10

Alicia rolled over to the sound of the phone ringing. She tried opening her eyes but she was too comfortable and warm. A small part of her brain knew that she should still be angry with Adam for some reason but she didn't want to be angry right now. She just wanted to snuggle more deeply into the sheets and into his chest.

She heard his voice and wanted him to hurry up and finish the phone call. Number one, it was disturbing her. And number two, she was hoping that she could tease him into making love to her once he hung up the phone.

"Dammit!" Alicia heard him say moments before the phone was slammed down into the cradle. Suddenly, he was hopping out of bed and pulling on a pair of jeans.

"What's going on?" she asked, pushing her hair out of her face.

"There's been a break in at the office. A fire was started," he said grimly, pulling a tee-shirt over his head and slipping his feet into a pair of running shoes, not even bothering with socks.

"Oh, Adam! I'm sorry. What can I do?" she asked, sitting up and getting out of bed herself. She rushed over to her dresser and pulled on a pair of jeans, noticing that she still had her shirt and bra on from the day before. She didn't take the time to wonder about it, too concerned with Adam's crisis.

"Nothing," he said, his voice deep with the remnants of sleep. "I want you to stay here. I don't know what is going on but Jim suspects that the fire might have been deliberate."

"Why?" she asked, continuing to dress, pulling on a pair of shoes. "Who would do something like that and why would they?"

Adam stopped for a moment, debating how much to tell her. This wasn't the best way to admit he'd made a mistake. But the truth would come out sooner or later. "The fire was started in the accounting department, with all the archived invoices." He took a deep breath before continuing. "Jim thinks that the person who embezzled money from the company wanted to cover their trail since the investigation was started up again."

He walked over to her and placed a quick, hard kiss on her open mouth. "Let me find out what is going on and I'll be back here. You'll still be here, won't you?" he asked, his dark eyes looking into her blue ones intently. "I'll explain everything when I get back."

Alicia's hand rose to her lips where he'd just kissed her. It felt like the whole world was becoming brighter and prettier. "Yes. Of course I'll be here," she said softly.

"Good. I'll be back as soon as I can."

Alicia watched him leave, then looked at the clock. It was only three o'clock in the morning. She knew she'd fallen asleep about midnight.

Her book! She remembered falling asleep on the sofa. Where was her book?

She ran out to the living room and saw her laptop, sitting closed on the coffee table. She blushed, wondering if he'd read her story. She certainly hoped not. But then, if he had, did he like it? Was it worthwhile?

Alicia pushed those thoughts away. She didn't care if he liked it. She walked back into the bedroom and stepped into the shower, wanting to be revived when he walked back in. Coffee! She knew Adam would need coffee. Good grief, she did herself! What time was it? She looked over at the clock and read the dial. It wasn't even five o'clock in the morning! She considered going back to bed but she was already up and extremely worried about Adam. If it were only his company, she would be upset. But if someone were running around the office setting fires, that meant he might be in danger.

Damn the man! If he hurt himself before she had a chance to tell him she loved him, she would be very angry with him. She didn't even consider the idea that something worse than only being hurt could be a possibility. The tightening around her chest at the "hurt" idea was too painful. If he died.....Alicia stopped her mind from going in that direction. There was no use in traipsing around horrible, impossible thoughts. No one could hurt Adam. He was too huge, too strong, too...invincible.

Alicia hurriedly dumped coffee grounds into the coffee maker then pressed the button to start the water. Her fingers were shaking and she covered her face with her hands, praying that nothing would happen to him. He was her life and if the only position he wanted her in was his mistress, well she'd be here for as long as that lasted.

When it was over? Well, she'd deal with that misery when it came. No use borrowing pain when it wasn't necessary.

The coffee finally finished brewing and she poured herself a cup, then took it out to the terrace, watching the sun rise over the city and river, her mind completely occupied with wondering what was happening and praying that he would walk in the door and tell her that everything was okay.

When the sun was finally over the city, she sighed and drained the last of her coffee. Deciding that this was pointless, she went back inside and turned on the television. Sure enough, there was a story on the news about the fire but no mention about where it was started or why. Was someone trying to hide evidence against them? If they'd embezzled money, would they be smart enough to hide it? How could anyone be stupid enough to leave a paper trail of that kind of a theft? But how could they not? Her father had been caught because of a paper trail which was one of the reasons she'd always shied away from e-mail correspondence whenever possible.

The noise coming from the foyer startled her since she'd been lost in concentration. "Adam?" she called out, placing her coffee cup on the table in front of her.

There was silence. Alicia frowned. Had she imagined the sound? It was possible. She turned around and watched the television for a few more minutes, hoping there would be an update to the fire or the investigation. But something tickled her senses and she couldn't ignore the idea that someone had actually entered the penthouse. Was she imagining things?

Alicia stood up and brought her coffee cup into the kitchen, turning off the television as she walked by and listened carefully. There were no other sounds in the large, airy space but she just couldn't get the idea out of her mind that she wasn't alone.

A strange sense stole over her and she walked into the bedroom to find her shoes. She'd taken them off when she'd gone to shower but knew that they were right there. She wanted to get out of here as quickly as possible. Something wasn't right, she just knew it.

As she walked to the bedroom, she looked around. Nothing was out of place, there were no movements she couldn't identify. Everything looked calm and where it should be. But she pulled on her sneakers quickly.

As she bent over to pull on the heel, she heard the movement a moment before she felt the pain shoot through her skull. Then blackness.

Chapter 11

When Alicia awoke, she was sitting on the bed, her hands tied together and her feet tied at her ankles. She wasn't gagged, so that was something. Ignoring the pain shooting through her skull, she looked around, fighting down the panic that threatened to overwhelm her. Her eyes frantically searched for the person who could have broken in and hit her over the head. How could anyone have gotten through security? Not only was there a guard down at the basement entrance as well as the front door, no one could get onto any of the floors, especially this one at the top, without a special key. The elevators wouldn't even work unless the key was turned in the lock. Then a code had to be entered.

Alicia didn't like the answers that came to mind as she reviewed all the layers of security someone would have to get through in order to get to her. That would mean that someone more skilled, and probably more ruthless, was in the apartment. Not that she liked the idea of a run of the mill burglar.

"Where's the money!" an angry female voice shouted from one of the other bedrooms.

A moment later, Nancy Peterson's angry form came through the bedroom door. "Good! I'm glad you're finally awake. You wouldn't have liked the way I would wake you up. Now tell me where this bastard keeps all of his money. I've already been through the library and office but I don't have time to search the whole bloody place. It is too large! So just tell me and no one gets hurt."

"Nancy?" Alicia asked, horrified at the image of her former manager. Gone was the professional, calm woman who had run the accounting department with humor and flair. That woman had always been impeccably dressed and polite, never raising her voice to anyone.

The termagant now standing in Adam's bedroom, brandishing a pistol in the air as if she was about to explode was not that other woman. Her hair was falling out of the pony tail she'd hurriedly pulled it into at some point, her jeans were covered in some sort of black soot and she had several tears in the tee-shirt that was hanging loose from her jeans on one side, while tucked in on the other.

"Of course it is me. Who did you expect? Santa Clause?"

"What are you doing?" Alicia asked, wanting to calm the older woman down slightly.

Nancy's eyes widened. "You don't know? You mean that bastard you're sleeping with didn't tell you?" The laughter that emanated from the woman could only be classified as demented. "What a hoot!" she said, bursting into a fresh wave of laughter. "And all this time, I thought he'd blamed you for the stolen money. That was the plan, after all. When you disappeared after your call to the boss's office, I was sure I was out of the heat," she explained, putting the gun down on the top of the dresser and pulling out the first drawer. "Good grief, this man has some nice clothes," she said absently, pulling out a pair of silk boxers and examining them.

Turning back to Alicia, she smiled conspiratorially. "So what's the great man like in bed? Hmmm?" Her eyes were bright, flashing something Alicia didn't understand. "Is he a dynamo? He's a bastard to be sure, but he's a handsome one. He's probably really good, isn't he?" she enthused, pulling out another pair of Adam's underwear.

Alicia couldn't answer. She was too terrified of the woman but also determined to not reveal her personal life with Adam.

Eventually, Nancy realized that she was talking frantically but not getting any response. She turned back to face Alicia. "So? What's the scoop?"

Alicia only glared at the crazy woman. "None of your business, Nancy."

Nancy's face reddened and she looked like she was about to do something violent. But then her eyes dimmed slightly and she shrugged her shoulders. "Okay, keep your secrets. I'm sure he's probably pathetic if you're still his lover. Look at you! You weren't even smart enough to know you were being framed!" And the hysterical laughter started again.

Nancy calmed and came towards the bed to look around the bedroom. "Fortunately, I'm not interested in sex with the man. I just want his money. So spill it woman. Where does he keep his loads of dough? I'm sure he has a personal stash somewhere in this mansion on top of the building. No one with this much money lives without cash. And I need it fast."

"I have no idea where Adam keeps his money, or even if he keeps it around here."

"Why the hell not?" she screeched, rushing over to the end of the bed, her eyes back to being lit by some inner hell.

"Because it is none of my business. It isn't my money." Alicia was terrified but trying to remain calm.

"So what? Every whore knows where her pimp's wad of cash is! Are you saying you're not even a good enough whore to get additional money from the sucker?"

"Nancy, perhaps if you told me what you needed the money for, I could ask Adam for a loan. He's very understanding," she lied, trying to come up with anything that would calm the woman down. She was obviously not the most stable character.

"Shut up! I don't want a loan," she screeched, the gun flailing in the air above her head. "I just want to get out of this town and hide somewhere until all this mess has cleared out." She looked around, searching for other hiding places. "Why are you here anyway? Shouldn't you be out spending his money? I've been waiting for you outside the building for the past three days. I saw the bastard leave and just assumed you'd be on your way out the door right after him." Nancy turned to smile back at Alicia. "I know I would be out spending his lovely money as fast as they could print it. But he wouldn't even notice, would he? The man has more money than he can probably count."

Nancy turned around and leaned the gun against her chin, thinking, her eyes darting around the room. They lit suddenly and she raced over to the walls. "Pictures! Why didn't I think of that!" she said, ripping the lovely oil paintings and stunning photographs off the wall. They tumbled to the floor, the glass shattering in the process.

She worked her way through the bedroom, then left and Alicia could hear her going through the rest of the penthouse, pictures crashing to the floor over and over again. Alicia frantically worked at the rope holding her hands but she was only rubbing the skin raw and had no success in even loosening the knot before Alicia heard yet another frustrated screech and Nancy stormed back into the bedroom. "Where the hell is his money?" she demanded.

Alicia shook her head, wishing she could think of something to say that would calm her down. "I imagine he keeps his money in the bank but that's just an assumption. I've never asked him."

"But you have credit cards, don't you?"

This wasn't the way things were supposed to go, Alicia thought to herself. "Yes. I suppose."

"You suppose?" Nancy asked, stunned to the point of her mouth hanging open slightly. "What do you mean, 'suppose'? Either you do or you don't."

"I do, but they are to the various stores. I don't just have a regular credit card," she explained.

"You have a cash card, don't you?"

"No, I'm sorry, Adam didn't give me one."

"How do you get your hands on his money then?" she asked, Nancy's eyes flashing frustrated fire.

"I don't. There's no need for me to have any cash. I'm sorry, Nancy, but I don't think there's anything I can do to help you. There's some jewelry on the table though," Alicia said quickly when Nancy started to lift the gun in her direction. "It isn't much, but it might help you get out of New York," she said.

Nancy sneered but looked over at the dressing table. As the older woman looked it over, Alicia worked at the knot with all her might. She'd have bruises but she'd created just a small amount of wriggle room in the rope. Maybe, if she could have just a few more moments, she could ....

It wasn't good enough. Nancy swung around and tossed the gold chains onto the bed. "You mean this is all that cheap bastard has given you? Haven't you been with him for almost two months?" Nancy laughed harshly. "You must not be very good in the sack if he hasn't given anything else to you."

"There are gold cufflinks in his drawer somewhere," Alicia said, panicking as Nancy grew more and more agitated.

Nancy's head swung around and she looked at the drawers she'd just gone through. "Where?"

"I'm not sure," Alicia said. "I don't watch him get dressed. I just know they are there."

As Nancy bent down, Alicia knew this might be her only chance. She stood up as quickly as she could and grabbed the brass lamp beside the bed with her still tied hands. Gripping it tightly, she rushed over to where her former friend was bent over, searching frantically through the drawers. With a sudden crash, Alicia jammed the lamp down over the woman's head.

For what seemed like a long moment, Alicia watched in horror as Nancy looked up. But then, as if in slow motion, the woman toppled to the floor, her eyes closed and the awful gun sitting benignly on the top of the dresser.

Seconds later, the police swarmed into the bedroom, guns drawn and Alicia couldn't take the stress any longer. Her hands were hurting and she simply dropped to the floor in a heap, letting the tears stream down her face. She felt the strong arms wrap around her as Adam lifted her into his arms, gently carrying her out of the bedroom while the police handcuffed the still unconscious woman.

"Adam!" Alicia cried, her still tied hands going around his neck. She was shaking all over, her body reacting after the fact to the situation and she was unable to control that reaction as shock set in. "Adam, you're here!"

"Yes, my love. I'm here. I'm sorry I left you alone. Are you okay?" he asked, pulling her hands over his head again and making short work of the tight knot. He gently rubbed her raw, scraped wrists before pulling her into his arms again.

"I'm fine now," she said, but she couldn't stop the tears or the shivering. "I'm sorry," she said.

Adam's laughter was soft, deep and infinitely reassuring. "You're sorry?" he asked. "I leave you alone with a mad woman and you're apologizing."

Alicia pulled back so she could wipe her eyes. "I'm sorry I can't stop crying. I'm sorry I'm being so emotional."

"You can't know how terrified I was when we figured out who had set the fire. When the police couldn't find her, I got a bad feeling in my gut and had to get home to you. When I found the front desk guard downstairs unconscious, I knew something was terribly wrong," he explained. "I called the police. Thankfully, they were already on their way or there would have been no way they would have stopped me from getting up here to you."

"Really?" she asked, the fear of the morning fading as the fear of what he was telling her moved in. "So Nancy was the one who embezzled all the money?" she asked, pulling back, terrified that he would not want her anymore.

"Yes. I started the investigation last week again. Too many things didn't add up."

Alicia nodded her head, but she couldn't look at him. The panic of being attacked was gone, replaced by a newer, worse panic.

"So I guess this whole mistress thing is over." Alicia's worst fears were now coming true. It would be over and Adam wouldn't want her anymore. The revenge was done.

"Yes." Adam stood up and ran his fingers through his hair. He glanced around the penthouse and then down at her. "Alicia, I know this isn't the time or the place and you've had probably the worst morning of your life. But I'm sorry, I won't let you go," he told her. With two quick strides, he was back in front of her, kneeling down and taking her hands gently within his strong ones. "Alicia, this can't be the end of it. I think you care for me and if it is only a small amount of the feelings I have for you, then I'm not going to let you walk out of here, walk out on us."

Alicia's teary eyes looked up into his dark, intense ones. "What are you saying?"

Adam pulled her into his lap. "I'm saying that I love you and I know I can make you feel the same way. If you'll just give me a chance to overcome these past two months, I promise I'll try and start over with you."

Alicia's eyes teared up again, but they were tears of joy and not of sadness or fear. "You love me?" she whispered, afraid she'd misunderstood him.

"Yes. And I think you care for me."

"But...how?" she asked.

Adam moved away from her, shoving his hands into his pockets. "That first night...at the party," he started off, "well, it was incredible. And I couldn't get you out of my mind. I'd had private investigators searching everywhere for you but they just came up with dead ends. So when Jim came to me and showed me your picture and all the evidence, well, I guess I just went a little crazy." He smiled but it was more of a grimace. "I had to have you again. And since you'd already slipped away from me once, I had to figure out how to keep you here with me for as long as it took to get you out of my system."

She took a deep, shuddering breath. "And did it work?" she asked.

Adam laughed harshly. "Hell no," he said. "You just got more and more under my skin. I don't know when it happened, but somehow,

I fell in love with you. And now that the investigation has shown that you weren't the person I originally accused you of, you're going to run from me as fast as you can, aren't you?" he asked, turning away.

Alicia smiled through the tears of happiness. She watched his strong, muscular back flex as if he were working through something in his mind but couldn't quite get it fixed.

"I'll be running, but into your arms," she said softly. "If what you said was still true," she hesitated. Alicia looked down at the carpet, terrified that she'd misunderstood.

Adam swung around, looking at her face. "Alicia?" he demanded. "Are you telling me what I think you're saying?"

"That I'm in love with you?" she asked, shrugging her shoulders.

The breath was knocked out of her system as strong arms swooped her up and carried her to the sofa. Adam's mouth covered hers, his body touching her everywhere as he kissed her. "I love you," he said before covering her mouth with his again.

The cough behind them slowly broke into their consciousness. Adam pulled his mouth away reluctantly but his arms continued to hold her firmly, protectively. "Yes, officer?" he asked, not the slightest bit embarrassed that he was almost making love with Alicia while a crazy woman was carted out of his home.

"I'm sorry to disturb this reunion, but I need to get Ms. Morgan's statement."

Adam reluctantly let her go, chuckling at her face that was flaming with embarrassment. But he sat beside her the whole time the man wrote and asked questions. Two hours later the cleaning crew, the police and even the reporter that had tried to sneak up to his penthouse were gone. Adam closed the door and looked at the tiny woman sitting on the sofa.

"You can't go back on your word, you know," he said, pulling her into his arms. "You're going to have to marry me now."

Alicia laughed. It was so like him to tell her what to do instead of asking, proposing in the traditional way. There wasn't a traditional bone in Adam's body, nor would she want it any other way. "Fine. But you're going to have to have children with me and promise to love me for at least the next fifty years. None of this silly celebrity or wealthy divorces, Adam," she admonished.

"Fifty years, huh?" he asked, taking both of her hands in his and pulling her up into his arms. "That's awfully demanding, you know."

"Yes. I know. I learned it from the best," she tossed back at him.

Adam laughed deeply, his white teeth flashing at her as he pulled her into his arms. "Okay. But I want lots of children," he said. "And they all have to have soft, blue eyes just like you."

"What if they are boys?" she asked, laughing at his sweet words.

"No boys," he said. "They are too stubborn," he said and tossed her into his arms, carrying her into the bedroom.

A message from Elizabeth:

The title of this story used to be "The Billionaire's Terms; Prison or Passion". At the time that I released this book, I loved the title. However, more than a decade later, the title and some of the scenes made me uncomfortable. I hope that this story reflects our current world a bit better and that it gave you a small bit of enjoyment. If you wouldn't mind, could you leave a review? Return to the book page and leave a review – and I thank you!

As usual, if you don't want to leave feedback in a public forum, feel free to e-mail me directly at elizabeth@elizabethlennox.com. I answer all e-mails personally, although it sometimes takes me a while. Please don't be offended if I don't respond immediately. I tend to lose myself in writing stories and have a hard time pulling my head out of the book.

Elizabeth

Keep scrolling for an excerpt to "The Sheik's Secret Twins!

Excerpt from The Sheik's Secret Twins
Now Available!

In the back of her mind, Siri heard Linda answer the door, but the mumbled greetings didn't break her concentration.

"Uh, Siri?" Linda called out.

"Tell them I'm not here," she called back, knowing that whoever it was could hear her comments but still hoping they would be discouraged.

"Um...I'm not sure this guy is going to take no for an answer."

That got through to Siri and she glanced up from her book. When she saw the tall man in the dark suit standing in her kitchen, the only other area besides the den and the two bedrooms which were on opposite sides of the den, Siri jumped up, dumping her books and notes all over the orange, shag carpet.

"Oh!" she cried out and looked down at the papers, then back up at the gorgeous man who was looking at her with a blank expression on his face. He looked scarier, more intimidating, in the bright afternoon sunshine. And much, much taller!

She pulled the pen out of her hair, wishing she'd pulled on something better than leggings and an old tee shirt which had definitely seen better days and only came down to her waist. "Sorry," she said and grabbed Linda's boyfriend's shirt which was draped over the back of the only other chair in the apartment. "I wasn't expecting anyone today. We were just studying."

"I'm sorry to interrupt," the man replied with a slight accent which Siri couldn't place immediately. "I thought perhaps we might be formally introduced since we had such an amusing evening last night."

Siri had to laugh despite her nervousness at this extremely large man in her apartment. "It wasn't so funny towards the end, but he did serve as a good amusement factor, didn't he?"

Malik took a step forward, his eyes looking over her beautiful skin for signs of abuse. "He didn't hurt you, did he? I know that you confronted him at the end, and I apologize for not being there to stop him if things became physical."

She looked up at him curiously. "It wasn't your responsibility to ensure my safety, but I appreciate the thought. I can take care of myself," she claimed.

Malik stopped his laughter, but only just in time. This woman who barely reached his shoulder thought she could handle an angry man with his pride wounded in front of his future employer? "I'm glad to hear it." He stepped back and smiled. "I would like to take you out to dinner myself, if you have the time."

Siri was startled and not sure how to respond. She looked to Linda who was just as awestruck. Regrouping quickly so she didn't appear so ridiculous, she replied, "I'm flattered, but I really don't think that I'm I your league," she stated softly, wishing that she could be in his league. This man was hunk material, but also terrifying for some reason.

Linda really didn't like Siri's response and stepped forward. "She'd be delighted," she contradicted. "What time and where should she meet you?" she asked, already picking up a pen and notebook and writing something down on it.

Malik glanced at the cute redhead who interceded on his behalf, appreciating her efforts. "Eight o'clock, tomorrow night? I'll pick you up here."

Linda nodded, ignoring Siri's attempt to contradict her. "That sounds perfect, " she said, nodding her head for emphasis. "Here's Siri's cell phone number in case anything comes up. And she'll be ready tomorrow at eight."

The tall, gorgeous man took the paper and bowed slightly, handing the paper to one of the large, bulky men behind him without even glancing at it. "I look forward to our evening. And I will work hard to ensure that I don't mistake my philosophers since you apparently are so well versed in their doctrines."

With that, he stepped out of the apartment and closed the door, leaving behind two stunned women who looked at each other as if they'd just been invited to a royal ball.

"Who was that man?" Linda asked, when she remembered to close her mouth, her whole body showing her excitement for Siri's new man.

Siri shrugged, still staring at the now closed door. "I have no idea. He was at the table next to ours last night and we looked at each other every time Gary said something stupid but I don't know his name. And I couldn't even guess where he's from since I couldn't place his accent."

Linda wasn't excited any longer. She was actually looking a bit worried now. "And you're going out with him? Is that safe?"

Siri turned to glare at her roommate, astonished that she was asking that question now after Linda had just accepted the date despite Siri's rejection. "Not really," she said with emphasis, raising an eyebrow. "But did I have a choice? Not really!"

Linda laughed and flopped back down on the sofa, her worry dissipating just as easily as it had appeared. "Well, it's about time you got out and explored a little. Have a bit of adventure tomorrow night with your mystery guy. He looks yummy, so enjoy it!"

"I might enjoy it more if I knew his name."

At that moment, her cell phone rang and she looked down at the tiny screen. It was an unknown number, but something told her to answer the call anyway. "Hello?" she answered warily.

"I think I forgot to tell you my name," a deep voice said over the phone.

"Yes, we were just mentioning that," she replied, glancing at Linda who was watching her eagerly.

"I'm Malik," he explained. "And I'm very glad to meet you, Siri."

She hesitated to ask, actually afraid of the answer but knowing she had to find out anyway. "How did you find out who I am?"

"I have a few resources."

"And how do you know where I live?"

"Same resources. I promise I'm not a stalker. Just consider me a man interested in getting to know a beautiful woman. I'll see you tomorrow night."

Siri glanced at her phone, then at Linda. "His name is Malik and he has 'resources'," she explained to her curious roommate.

"He has a lot more than resources," Linda replied with a grin before once more diving back into her books.

Made in United States
North Haven, CT
19 February 2023

32850452R00078